THE CURSE

OF IMHOTEP

A James Acton Thriller

Also by J. Robert Kennedy

James Acton Thrillers

The Protocol
Brass Monkey
Broken Dove
The Templar's Relic
Flags of Sin
The Arab Fall
The Circle of Eight
The Venice Code
Pompeii's Ghosts
Amazon Burning
The Riddle
Blood Relics
Sins of the Titanic

Saint Peter's Soldiers
The Thirteenth Legion
Raging Sun
Wages of Sin
Wrath of the Gods
The Templar's Revenge
The Nazi's Engineer
Atlantis Lost
The Cylon Curse
The Viking Deception
Keepers of the Lost Ark
The Tomb of Genghis Khan

The Manila Deception
The Fourth Bible
Embassy of the Empire
Armageddon
No Good Deed
The Last Soviet
Lake of Bones
Fatal Reunion
The Resurrection Tablet
The Antarctica Incident
The Ghosts of Paris
No More Secrets
The Curse of Imhotep

Dylan Kane Thrillers

Rogue Operator
Containment Failure
Cold Warriors
Death to America
Black Widow

The Agenda
Retribution
State Sanctioned
Extraordinary Rendition

Red Eagle
The Messenger
The Defector
The Mole
The Arsenal

Just Jack Thrillers
You Don't Know Jack

Templar Detective Thrillers

The Templar Detective
The Parisian Adulteress
The Sergeant's Secret

The Unholy Exorcist
The Code Breaker

The Black Scourge
The Lost Children
The Satanic Whisper

Kriminalinspektor Wolfgang Vogel Mysteries
The Colonel's Wife   Sins of the Child

Delta Force Unleashed Thrillers

Payback
Infidels
The Lazarus Moment

Kill Chain
Forgotten
The Cuban Incident

Rampage
Inside the Wire
Charlie Foxtrot

Detective Shakespeare Mysteries
Depraved Difference   Tick Tock   The Redeemer

Zander Varga, Vampire Detective
The Turned

THE CURSE
OF IMHOTEP

A James Acton Thriller

J. ROBERT KENNEDY

UnderMill PRESS

ISBN: 9781998005499

First Edition

For Tina Turner.

Simply the best.

THE CURSE
OF IMHOTEP

A James Acton Thriller

"The wab-priest may give offerings to your ka. The wab-priests may stretch to you their arms with libations on the soil, as it is done for Imhotep with the remains of the water bowl."

Inscription found on Ancient Egyptian tomb, c. 1391-1353 BCE, written over 1300 years after Imhotep's death.

"Social media is a very, very powerful tool. It also gives power to tools."

Chris Young

PREFACE

The irresponsible use of social media is a bane to society that has divided communities and countries, polarizing people into opposite sides of issues, and eliminating the middle ground. This binary society is at a dangerous risk of collapse, and has already resulted in untold deaths.

Suicide is the second leading cause of death among teenagers, and heavy use of social media (a few hours a day) has been linked to an increased risk of our youth taking their lives due to cyberbullying and other online cruelty.

Today's obsession with gaining followers, likes, shares, and that all-important "viral" status is pushing commonsense to the wayside in exchange for a chance at what is no longer the infamous fifteen minutes of fame, but a hoped-for lifetime of relevancy based on validation from people never met.

The chance at gaining followers is so tempting, that rules are broken, laws are violated, and simple good sense is ignored, affecting all aspects of our lives.

And what would happen if such a person, obsessed with the goal of being famous for being famous, were to be unleashed on an unsuspecting archaeological dig site?

Quite possibly scores of dead, all tying back to one fool and her phone.

Sudan

Three Days from Now

Archaeology Professor Laura Palmer's shoulders slumped in defeat. She pushed to her feet then raised her blood-stained hands over her head, slowly turning to face the armed men surrounding her. It was a true out of the frying pan and into the fire moment. What she would give for just one thing to go right today. Today was supposed to be a high point of her career. The discovery was so monumental, it could rewrite history, and at a minimum, fill in a lot of blanks that had stumped scholars for centuries.

But instead, everything had gone horribly wrong, and now she stood in the middle of the desert with blood literally soaking her hands, belonging to men whom the government here would likely claim she murdered. And just when she thought she had escaped their clutches, she was once again surrounded, this time by greater numbers with no hope in hell of escape this time.

But these men weren't military. They appeared to be Bedouins. Were they her enemy? Were they here to kill her, or kidnap her and demand a ransom be paid for her safe return?

Or were they merely here to help?

Nobody said anything, the tension growing among those who surrounded her. A camel spat to her left and her head spun toward the sound. She spotted a group of women holding the reins of half a dozen of the beasts of burden. She made eye contact with one of the women who smiled at her. These people might not be her enemy after all. Or they could be fanatics. There was only one way to find out.

She directed her attention at the man who appeared to be in charge, one of the oldest there, and the only one not pointing a gun directly at her. She prayed he spoke Arabic. "My name is Professor Laura Palmer, and I need your help, otherwise a lot of innocent people are going to die."

South of Ancient Philae
July 13, 1939

Bernhardt Stoltz, professor of antiquities at the German Archaeological Institute, stared at the hieroglyphics over the massive cover stone that stood before him. *Hauptsturmführer* Heidrich Wirth, a constant thorn in his side and an SS officer, stood impatiently beside him as he finished the translation.

"Well, what does it say?"

Stoltz could barely contain his excitement as he flipped through his notes to confirm what he already knew. He found the symbol he was seeking and compared it to what he had written, then again to what was carved above the cover stone.

"It says, 'Here lies Imhotep, honored friend to Pharaoh Djoser. Eternal damnation awaits any who disturb his slumber.'"

Wirth laughed. "These Egyptians are so melodramatic. Were they really so primitive to believe such nonsense would scare anyone?"

Stoltz tensed. He was sick of the man's attitude. The disrespect shown to the local Egyptian workers was one thing, but to criticize one of the greatest cultures the world had ever known was beyond ignorant. The man was here to represent the interests of the Third Reich. While the dig was under the control of the Institute, everything in Germany was ultimately under the control of the Führer, and that meant either Gestapo in leather trench coats, party members in brown shirts, or SS in their Hugo Boss-produced jet-black uniforms.

He hated what his country had become, though in today's Germany, one kept one's head down if one wanted to survive. War hadn't broken out yet, but he was quite certain it would anytime now. It was inevitable, and he was happy to be in Egypt, sheltered from most of the nonsense, though not all of it.

This very dig was part of Hitler's madness.

And it was time for a little fun with the overzealous young officer. "You seem to forget, Hauptsturmführer, that while you may disrespect the achievements of the Ancient Egyptians, our Führer certainly doesn't."

Wirth stared at him, clearly uneasy. "What do you mean?"

"Why are we here? Why are our archaeologists spread across the globe? We've been tasked to find ancient relics that might assist in the war that is to come. Clearly, our Führer believes that ancient cultures like the Egyptians had powers that have been lost to time. If you laugh at their beliefs, then you laugh at his."

Wirth took an involuntary step backward, his head shaking. "I meant no disrespect. I…" He struggled to find the words to recover but failed.

Stoltz suppressed a smile. "Don't worry, Hauptsturmführer, your trivializing of the Führer's beliefs won't make it into any report I write."

Wirth's shoulders slumped, his head dropping onto his chest. "Thank you, Professor. I am in your debt."

"Yes, you are." Stoltz stepped back and gestured at the cover stone. "I think it's time we met Imhotep, don't you?"

Wirth nodded then hesitated. "But what of the curse?"

Stoltz laughed. "Hauptsturmführer, even I don't believe in curses, nor do I think our Führer does. We've been tasked to find relics, not words." He turned to the supervisor of the Egyptian workers. "Let's get this stone out of the way," he said in perfect Arabic.

The man bowed and barked orders, half a dozen men rushing into the small corridor of the crypt, discovered by accident when the ever-shifting sands of the Sahara exposed a small corner of the structure buried for millennia. Grunting echoed through the narrow passage as the work crew struggled, the bottom of the cover stone wedged into a keyway that held it in place. Stone scraping on stone indicated success was at hand, the massive obstacle moving barely an inch, enough for a puff of pulverized stone to erupt as one side of the keyway disintegrated. One of the workers rushed forward and hammered a wood wedge between the stone and the floor, preserving their slight progress.

The men eased off, gasping for breath before the supervisor ordered them back into position. More echoes of toiling filled Stoltz's ears with excitement as the stone slowly rolled to the side, a cheer erupting as it cleared the keyway. He held his tongue, allowing the men to once again rest rather than order them back to work to satisfy his eagerness. While they were laborers being paid a pittance by German standards, they still deserved his respect, and respected men always worked harder than the disrespected.

He just prayed Wirth kept his mouth shut.

The order to resume was once again given, and the men positioned themselves, the eagerness of the crew evident, and Stoltz thanked God that these highly superstitious men couldn't read ancient hieroglyphics. Otherwise, the entire dig site would empty out of their local workforce. The stone rolled aside with relative ease now, and he could have sworn that as the seal was broken to the chamber, it gasped, an odd mustiness rolling through the opening and into the corridor.

His pulse drummed in his ears, and he couldn't help but think back to Howard Carter and what had happened to so many of his team after they discovered the tomb of King Tutankhamun. He ordered the workers outside before turning on his flashlight to see what lay in the inky blackness, untouched by the torchlight surrounding them. There could be nothing, merely another empty chamber, or there could be untold treasures that might tempt the workforce that far outnumbered them, to slaughter their German masters and loot a piece of history.

He waited for the last local to disappear up the steps, leaving him alone with Wirth and two of his grad students. He drew a deep breath and held it, clicking on his flashlight and aiming it into the darkness. He played it across the floor, cautiously stepping forward, when something was caught by the beam.

And he gasped at a pair of hollow eyes staring back at him.

Cairo, Egypt

Present Day, Three Days Earlier

"Can we cancel his ticket? I think *I* want to sleep in here."

"Don't even think about it," replied Archaeology Professor James Acton's wife, Laura Palmer. "Right now, I'm more excited to see him than you."

Acton gave her a look. "If I didn't know you better, I'd say you were joking, but I think you actually mean that."

She grinned. "I do."

"Thank God he's twenty years my senior or I might be jealous."

"You're ten years older than me. I obviously like older men."

"Fine. I'll make sure you two get some alone time. With this air conditioning, though, you won't exactly be sweating up the sheets."

"You're terrible."

"You're just discovering this now?"

"Yet I still somehow love you." She patted him on the cheek as they stepped back into the oppressive heat of a Cairo spring.

He groaned at the heat. "A night in our tent in this heat is definitely going to soak the sheets."

"I guess you'll have to get your fill the next few nights in the hotel."

He frowned. "That wasn't part of the deal. When I agreed to come here for a month instead of going to Peru with my dig, I was promised all kinds of lovin'."

"That was before we had this record heat wave. Last night in our tent was truly a Breakfast Club moment."

He eyed her, puzzled, then Judd Nelson's line echoed in his head and he grinned. "Oh, you mean when I gave you the hot—"

She held up a finger, cutting him off, nodding toward the rental agent rushing toward them. "We've got company. You keep your potty mouth to yourself."

He opened his mouth to say something else but thought better of it.

"So, does it meet your specifications?" asked the rental agent, who had insisted they call him Mo.

"It's perfect," said Laura. "Our friends will be thrilled."

"And you said you'll be picking it up in three days?"

"Yes, we'll be driving it down to our dig site, then should have it back seven days later."

"Excellent. And if you need an extension on that, just let me know. No one has it booked after you, yet."

"We'll let you know," said Acton.

Mo handed over a clipboard. "Just sign where the X's are, and she'll be ready for you in three days."

"With a full tank?"

"Absolutely. And the batteries fully charged."

Acton checked the hood to make certain there wasn't a leaping jungle cat signaling future headaches as Laura signed the paperwork. "You're sure you don't want to get two of them?"

"The only way I'm getting one for us is if I get one for all of our students."

He shrugged. "Sounds good to me, though I think they'll be pretty cramped."

She groaned. "You know what I mean."

"Yeah, yeah. We get to suffer along with our students."

"It's hardly suffering. Every one of those tents has a portable air conditioner. My dig site is luxurious compared to most, thanks to my brother's money." Her face clouded over with the mention of her brother, the events of Qatar still far too raw. He reached out and took her hand, giving it a gentle squeeze. She gave him a weak smile. Mo sensed something was amiss and shifted uncomfortably. Laura wiped the corner of her eyes. "Sorry about that. I recently lost my brother."

Mo clasped his chest. "You have my condolences. I recently lost my sister. If it's any comfort, it's true what they say. Time does indeed heal all wounds."

She smiled at the man. "Thank you." She inhaled sharply then expelled her lungs rapidly, her face brightening as if a switch had been thrown. "Enough of this. We've taken up too much of your time."

Mo gave them a copy of the rental agreement and shook their hands. "It's been a pleasure, and we'll see you in three days."

They headed for their Mercedes GLS 580 SUV, one of their dig site vehicles. Acton held out his hand. "I'll drive." Laura, who normally did the driving, handed over the keys without protest, indicating she was still upset. They climbed in and he started the engine, adjusting the vents to direct the air conditioning at strategic locations. He sighed with pleasure. "Man, that heat really gets to you when you're standing on concrete."

Laura broke out in sobs, leaning over the center console. He embraced her as she cried, gently stroking her head and back. These episodes were becoming less frequent and eventually would be a distant memory, but not today. It was why he had wanted to get Reading to the dig to help take her mind off things.

"I just wish I knew," she gasped. "I just wish I knew the truth. I just wish I knew for sure."

He kissed the top of her head. "I know, but it's better this way, and in time, when it no longer matters, we will know."

She sniffed hard then pulled away. He handed her a handkerchief and she dried her eyes then blew her nose before checking herself in the mirror. "Ugh, look at me. My eyes are all puffy and red. I look terrible."

He decided to lighten the mood. "Still the sexiest piece of ass on the continent."

"You're terrible."

"I thought we already established that fact."

She flipped the visor back and her shoulders sagged. "Sometimes I'm such a girl, crying at the drop of a hat."

Acton put the SUV in gear and pulled away. "Well, if that's the definition of being a girl, then I better mail in my man card. You know how I was after Mom died."

She smiled at him and squeezed his leg, saying nothing as he battled his own grief. Laura's phone rang and she pulled it from her pocket, her eyes narrowing. "It's the dig." She swiped her thumb and put it on speaker. "Hello?"

"Hello, Professor. It's Terrence."

Acton could hear the young man was tense. Laura picked up on it as well. "Has something happened?"

"Well, sort of."

Acton smiled as Jenny growled in the background, Terrence Mitchell's wife, also a student of Laura's, far more direct than her husband. "Just tell her what happened. The poor woman probably thinks somebody died."

"Well, somebody did die."

Laura gasped. "What?"

Even Acton tensed at the words that made no sense in the context as he currently understood it.

"Oh, Terrence, sometimes you're impossible. Now they think somebody died." Jenny's voice grew louder as she came closer to the phone. "Professor, nobody died. Everybody's fine. Nobody's hurt. There was no accident. But we did discover something that we're not sure what to do with, and we may need to get the authorities involved."

"What did you find?" asked Acton, still concerned even with the lack of context. And when Mitchell told them, his concern was justified.

"I'll be returning immediately," said Laura.

South of Ancient Philae

August 23, 1939

It was the discovery of a lifetime. Career-making. The temptation of the amateur would have been to hurriedly explore everything in the room, shoving aside the lid of the sarcophagus, tearing open the lids of the jars to see what was held inside. But he had kept his eagerness in check. It wasn't just the tomb for the revered Imhotep, designer of the world's first step pyramid, respected and pioneering physician in an era that most thought had no such thing, but also to almost a dozen other bodies strewn about. He had heard of the ancient practice where many of the pharaoh's servants would be killed and entombed with him to serve him in the afterlife, but Imhotep was just a man. He didn't gain his demigod status until centuries after his death.

And there was chaos among the bones, scratches in the stone suggesting those found near the cover stone had attempted to get out, the rest positioned as if they had sat around the tomb, accepting their fate. Most of the bodies were young, male and female, though those near

15

the entrance were older. Inside the sarcophagus, a simple stone affair with the standard writings identifying who was inside and their accomplishments during their lifetime, proved beyond a doubt that it was indeed Imhotep, his mummified remains remarkably well preserved.

The sarcophagus and the body were now in the back of a truck, along with scores of priceless treasures meant to provide for Imhotep in his afterlife, all now the property of the Third Reich. Everything had been cataloged, though the identity of whose tomb they had discovered hadn't been reported out of fear it might leak and the area could be overrun with cultists who worshipped a man now revered as a god.

The most curious thing was the stone tablet discovered resting on Imhotep's chest. It was clear from what had been etched into its surface that Imhotep's death had been anything but peaceful.

"Professor, there's something you need to see!" squawked the voice of one of his grad students over the radio.

He grabbed the handset. "What is it?"

"We've got a sandstorm behind us!"

Stoltz leaned out the window, craning his neck to see behind them, and gasped. The entire horizon billowed with sand, rapidly closing in on them. He turned back, staring at the long convoy that stretched out in front of them comprised of two dozen transport vehicles as well as half a dozen escort cars like he was in. The entire dig had packed up and left on orders from Berlin, despite his protests. There was still more to be discovered, but apparently war was imminent, and teams across the globe like his were being recalled.

It was so frustrating. They had made an incredible find, perhaps the greatest since King Tut, perhaps even more so, considering Tut was a minor figure in history. Imhotep was a legend, a man who had accomplished incredible things, building structures that still stood to this day. Tut was a boy who accomplished nothing of significance that history recorded. He could study what they had discovered and continue at the dig site for the rest of his career, yet his country was hell-bent on conquest, hell-bent on taking what wasn't theirs.

He was old enough to remember the *Weltkrieg*, the World War. It had been hell, and his country had been punished mercilessly for what its leaders had done. The overreach of the Treaty of Versailles was why the German people had turned to the Nazi Party with its promise to rebuild, to take back what had been lost, and to do away with the crippling reparations demanded by the victorious Allies.

But it was one thing to rebuild, to refuse to pay. It was an entirely different thing to go to war.

Yet again, the history was there, but their Führer appeared unwilling to learn from it. But none of that mattered. The orders had been given and they were on the road, completely exposed to the hellish fury approaching. He was responsible for all these people, and he was well aware of how deadly a storm such as this could be. He hadn't experienced one yet, though had read accounts of those who had, barely escaping with their lives, only to report how many others in their group hadn't.

He grabbed the map wedged between the seats and unfolded it. "We need to find shelter."

The route they were taking was traced out, and he ran his finger along it. He tapped their current location. Just ahead was the turn that would take them to the coast and the port with the ship set to transport them home. But just across the border into Sudan, there were hills with a gorge that might just protect them.

He held his radio to his lips. "This is Professor Stoltz. We have a storm coming in behind us. Rather than making the upcoming turn, we're going to continue straight on this road. It leads to a gorge where we can take shelter. Once the storm passes, we'll resume our regular route."

Acknowledgments came in from the various vehicles, and moments later, the driver pressed a little harder on the gas as the convoy ahead of them picked up speed while heads leaned out windows, the terrified eyes revealing what he already knew.

They wouldn't make it in time.

Cairo International Airport

Cairo, Egypt

Present Day

Acton smiled broadly as he spotted his good friend Hugh Reading clearing customs with his son Spencer. Reading had refused the offer of their private jet, the man never comfortable accepting expensive gestures. He understood why. He was the same. Archaeology professors weren't paid much and, until he met Laura, he had had no concept of what being rich truly meant. It wasn't a lot of zeros in a bank account, and it wasn't not worrying whether you could make the mortgage payment.

It was freedom.

It was power.

Freedom to do what you wanted when you wanted and how you wanted. And power not over people, unless of course that was your thing, but instead, power over uncertainty, over the daily troubles of the common man. When you had hundreds of millions of dollars, spending

19

twenty or thirty grand to send your private jet to pick up a friend and his son for a vacation in Egypt was as trivial as sending them an Uber.

The longer he was married to Laura, the more he found the real cost of things being forgotten. He simply enjoyed helping people, friends, family, and strangers alike, as did Laura. Their lifestyle was anything but ostentatious, though he supposed most on the outside would disagree, and perhaps they were right. It was just another example of how he was losing touch with what used to be his reality.

His grumpy old friend, however, had a firm grip on it, and had insisted on flying on a regular aircraft, though had acquiesced in letting them pay for the tickets.

Acton waved and Reading scowled as he walked toward him. Acton laughed, knowing exactly why his friend was giving him such a look, but decided to play dumb. "Bad flight?"

"You know bloody well it was a fantastic flight. You had us in first class. I said cheapest tickets possible."

"I'm pretty sure Mary got us a good deal."

Reading rolled his eyes as Spencer joined them, the young man excited. "I've never flown first class before. Thanks, Professor!"

Acton shook Spencer's hand, giving his father a look. "See? That's how you express gratitude."

"Bollocks."

Acton laughed, slapping his friend on the arm. Reading's eyes narrowed. "Where's Laura?"

"Plans have changed, I'm afraid. Something's happened at the dig site so she had to return."

Reading's scowl disappeared, instantly concerned about Laura, someone Acton was well aware the man deeply cared for as if she were his own daughter. "What's happened?"

Acton led them out of the terminal. "I'm not exactly sure yet. Apparently, they found a body at the bottom of an old well."

Spencer, a proud member of the London Police Service, immediately took an interest. "As in ancient remains or something more sinister?"

"Well, I have no idea if it's sinister, but it's definitely not ancient. Terrence called us because they were concerned they might need to call the authorities in, so she headed back yesterday afternoon."

Reading frowned. "That's a long drive alone, and she wouldn't be arriving until after dark."

Acton smiled. "Don't worry. I've already heard from her. She arrived at the dig, no problem. And she called this morning. She was just about to enter the well to see what was up. We'll probably be hearing from her any minute now. But in the meantime, I have a tour planned for us, but you'll have to put up with me playing tour guide rather than Laura and her sultry voice."

Spencer appeared genuinely disappointed with the prospect.

"No, we should head to the dig immediately," said Reading.

Acton opened the rear hatch of the SUV and helped load their luggage. "I'm sure it's nothing to worry about."

"It's a body," said Reading as Acton closed the hatch. "If you're already certain it's not ancient remains, then it has to be reported to the authorities, and that's going to mean local authorities. That means small-town Egyptian police. You do not want her dealing with them alone.

This is an extremely sexist society. I need to be there. My Interpol ID will stop most of the bullshit."

Acton frowned. His friend was right. Laura was such an incredibly capable woman that he rarely worried about her, but they had previous run-ins with Egyptian authorities and they rarely listened to a woman. They were liable to arrest everyone, throw them in a local jail to rot while they beat the so-called truth out of the students. He climbed behind the wheel, starting the engine. "You're right. I'm going to see if I can get your RV early, then we'll head directly there. We should be able to get there before nightfall."

"Do we have time for that?"

"We'll make time," replied Acton. "When this turns out to be much ado about nothing, I don't want to spend the next seven days with you bitching about the heat."

Spencer grinned from the back seat. "He's got you there."

Reading grunted. "We'll see how *you're* feeling after a couple of days. The British body wasn't built for it."

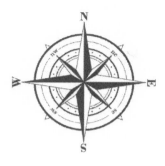

South of Ancient Philae

August 23, 1939

Stoltz sat in his seat, the wind howling around him, sand pelting the windows and the body of the car while the screams of panic from members of his archaeological team occasionally broke through the near ear-splitting fury of the storm. They had reached the gorge he had hoped would provide them with shelter, but instead, it could prove to be their tomb.

The storm had hit them hard, just short of the gorge the road passed through, quickly blinding them. A panicked radio call from the lead vehicle indicated they couldn't see a thing, and that they were slowing, a warning to those behind them. The gut-wrenching screeches of metal meeting metal indicated the warning had gone unheeded by some, and the entire convoy came to a rapid, unceremonious halt.

That had been half an hour ago.

He had given orders to shelter in place to wait things out, but he had never expected this. Sand was piling up around them, transports ahead already indicating it was reaching their doors, the gorge acting as a funnel, directing a massive amount of the desert picked up by the winds of the storm down upon the convoy.

This had been the wrong decision. He had killed them all. He peered out his window and cringed at the height of the sand, almost at the doors now. Soon he wouldn't be able to get out without breaking the window, and if the storm continued, even that might not be a possibility, the height of the impassible barrier building at least an inch every few minutes.

He closed his eyes.

Please, Lord, tell me what to do.

It was foolish to think he would get an answer. Prayers were never answered. He stared at the map then marked their location with an X. And made a decision. He folded it up and placed it inside his journal where he had documented the find and their current predicament, then tied it up, stuffing it inside his breast pocket. He turned to his driver sitting beside him, gripping the steering wheel with white knuckles.

"Give me your goggles."

"What?"

"Give me your goggles."

The corporal complied and Stoltz fit them in place, making certain the seal around his eyes was tight.

"You're not going out in that, are you?"

"I don't have a choice. If I don't go now, we'll be trapped."

"But you'll die out there for sure."

"Quite possibly. But our only hope of getting help is back there on the road. If I can make it, even if they find my body"—he patted the journal—"the map marks the spot where they can find you. Some of you may survive if you're discovered quickly enough, but right now, nobody knows where we are and these radios can't get a signal through the storm."

He bent down and tucked his pant legs into his socks, tightened his bootlaces, then turned up his collar and buttoned his jacket all the way up. He fit his gloves on over his sleeves then inspected himself for gaps.

The corporal cursed and reached into the back, pulling forward his kit. He handed over a gas mask. "Use this. It should hopefully allow you to breathe until the filter fills up with sand. Even then, you should still be able to catch your breath in the wind if you remove the filter."

"Good thinking." Stoltz removed the goggles then fit the gas mask in place. Breathing was immediately more difficult, though he was certain it would prove infinitely easier than what he was about to experience without it.

The corporal checked to make sure it was fit properly in place then extended his hand. "Professor, I should be coming with you, but I'm ashamed to admit I'm far too terrified."

Stoltz shook the man's hand. "You're not a coward, Corporal. You're merely not stupid enough to do what I'm about to attempt." He tapped the mask. "And besides, we only have one of these. Good luck."

"Good luck, Professor."

Stoltz shoved the door open, sand whipping into the cabin. He stepped out into the onslaught then slammed the door shut. He pushed against the wind, his hand tracing the edge of their car, a car he could no longer see. His fingers abruptly pressed against nothing, and he trudged forward slowly, leaving behind the shelter of the car and the convoy full of people and priceless history he was responsible for. And as he pushed through the rapidly accumulating sand, he quickly realized he had made a horrible mistake, and his mind couldn't help but recite the warning Hauptsturmführer Wirth had laughed off as superstitious nonsense.

Eternal damnation awaits any who disturb his slumber.

University College London Dig Site

Lower Nubia, Egypt

Present Day

Laura gripped the rope she dangled from in one hand, her free hand outstretched, using the walls of the ancient well to steady her descent. To the uninitiated, a dry well would seem to be of little interest to an archaeologist. After all, all it had once contained was water. But wells held secrets. Things were dropped accidentally in wells, things were hidden. Untold treasures could lie below, and every so often, something incredibly shocking could be found. Something that made no sense.

Terrence Mitchell, a trusted PhD candidate who ran the dig in her absence, had been excavating a well they had recently discovered buried in the sand, and then found something shocking. So shocking, there was no question of returning, leaving her husband to meet their good friend, Interpol Agent Hugh Reading.

Their friend had been lured to the desert with the promise of an air-conditioned trailer. He had been reluctant at first. In fact, he had downright refused it with a plethora of inappropriate comments about the combination of desert heat and his bollocks. But when his son had caught wind of the offer and asked if he could join him, he had changed his mind. Reading was desperate to rebuild his fractured relationship with his son who had spent most of his formative years being raised by Reading's ex-wife who poisoned the boy against his father.

James and their guests would be spending several days in Cairo so the young man could see some of the sights before joining the dig. She had been looking forward to the tour. Giza, the Sphinx, the Djoser Pyramid, there was so much to see here it was overwhelming at times, but if her grad student was correct in what he thought they had found, this could prove far more interesting in the short term than seeing what had stood for thousands of years, and would hopefully last for thousands more.

Her feet reached the bottom and she steadied herself. "All right, I'm down!" she called to those above, and the rope slackened. She unhooked it from her harness, her eyes already glued to the partially excavated find—a leathery corpse preserved in time by the sand that had entombed it, and the dry air of the Sahara. She shone her flashlight over the area then snapped several dozen photos with her phone before finally recording a video, preserving the state of the scene before she began her work.

She stood and peered above. "All right, send down the lamp!"

"On its way, Professor!" called Mitchell.

A lamp was lowered. She unhooked it, setting it opposite the remains, adjusting its legs for the uneven surface. She pressed the switch, activating it, and the narrow confines were flooded with light. She took more photos and another video, her excitement growing.

"Send down the bucket with my tools!"

Her request was acknowledged and moments later, she set to work gently removing some of the sand, revealing more of the man's clothing, confirming what Mitchell had already suspected—this was not the remains of somebody from thousands of years ago, but someone far more recent. She continued to document the find on her phone, discovering several pieces of splintered wood around the body. She twisted her head and smiled at the half-dozen faces peering down at her from above.

"I think the well was covered by wood at some point. I'm guessing sand accumulated on top of it, then this poor guy walked on it, probably without realizing what was under his feet. The wood broke, he fell in, then the sand buried him."

"What about his clothing?" asked Jenny.

"Twentieth century. Definitely not ancient Egyptian from the state of it. And what I've seen in the past with bodies discovered in these conditions, I'd say he's been here about a century."

She noticed the jacket had shoulder straps. It could mean nothing, lots of jackets had them, but it could indicate a uniform. She continued her excavation, concentrating on the left arm, some of it already exposed. She carefully brushed the sand into a scoop before emptying it into her bucket, repeating the process dozens of times before she spotted the top of an armband, a dark gray, probably once a sharp black. A hint of white was revealed with the next sweep, and her heart hammered as more of what she suspected it could be was exposed. She fell back on her haunches, bracing herself against the stone wall of the well, her mouth agape, her eyes wide with shock as what she had suspected was confirmed.

A Nazi swastika.

"It's a Nazi!" she shouted.

"What?" Mitchell sounded as shocked as she felt. "Are you sure?"

"He's either a Nazi or a guy with questionable judgment heading to a costume party. I'm going to continue excavating. One of you start looking into the history of this area. Were the Nazis here at any point? Don't forget pre-war. They had teams all over the place, including Egypt. Contact the German Archaeological Institute. They should have records on any of their digs in Egypt."

"I'll get right on it," replied Jenny.

She continued her painstaking work, forcing herself to control her excitement. What was a Nazi doing in this area? The only major find of any significance was hers, and there had been no evidence that it had been previously discovered in the past century. Certainly, if the Nazis had set up camp here at some point, her team would have found evidence of it, but they had found none.

Could he be military stationed here during the war, reported missing by his comrades after falling in the well? She dismissed the idea. This wasn't a military uniform. The only thing so far to indicate what this man was, was the armband. His upper torso was exposed now, revealing no additional military emblems, further confirming this wasn't a soldier. She noticed a rectangular bulge on the left side of his chest. She gently pressed against it to find there was something hard underneath. She carefully unbuttoned his jacket, documenting her progress, then reached inside, removing whatever it was the man had thought important enough to carry on his person.

Her heart raced as a leather-bound notebook was revealed, carefully tied up, a name handwritten across the cover.

Professor Bernhardt Stoltz.

The fact this belonged to a professor was exciting in itself, but what truly had the pulse pounding in her ears was the emblem in gold on the center of the cover, the emblem of the German Archaeological Institute. Could this man have been a scientist like her? Could he have been an archaeologist?

And if so, why would somebody of such importance have been left to die in a well, all alone?

South of Ancient Philae

August 23, 1939

Stoltz stared at the barren landscape in front of him. The storm had passed. He had made it. He had survived, though barely. The unrelenting wind had pummeled him for almost an hour, the gritty sand finding every minute gap in his clothing, and his skin felt raw in far too many places.

He tore the gas mask off and gasped in lungsful of air. The filter had quickly clogged, as his driver had predicted, and there was a moment of panic before he figured out how to remove it. He had still been able to breathe, though he had no idea how much sand he had actually swallowed while doing so.

He was exhausted, he was spent, but he was alive with a job to do. He reached for his radio, tucked inside his jacket, but it wasn't there. In a panic, his hands rapidly searched all over his body, coming up empty. He collapsed to his knees, battling the overwhelming urge to weep. He had fallen countless times during his ordeal, and on one of those occasions, the radio must have fallen loose. He twisted around, peering behind him, but it was useless. The landscape was unrecognizable, even his footprints long filled in.

His only hope of saving his team now was to find the road and pray someone would come across him. He confirmed he still had his journal tucked inside his inner breast pocket. If he could just make the road, even if he died on it, someone would eventually find him, read his last passage, and examine the map. His team would still be dead, but at least their bodies would be found and they would be given a proper burial. And the priceless treasures and the body of Imhotep himself would be recovered.

He pushed to his feet and dusted himself off as best he could, then pressed forward, taking a mouthful of water from his canteen and swishing it about, spitting out the grit before taking another large drink and swallowing. He trudged through the sand, peering ahead in the slowly fading sun, but couldn't find the road.

As he plodded onward, he soon realized he was facing two problems. One was the fact he was barely covering a couple of miles in an hour over the uneven surface, far less than what the convoy had been doing during their panicked escape attempt. The other was that so much sand had been deposited, not only might he never find the road, the likelihood of any traffic traversing what might be left was highly unlikely until it could be cleared, and he had no idea how efficient the Egyptians were at reopening roads after events like this.

He trudged on, the sun setting to his left until it could no longer be used as a guide. He stared up at the stars and found Polaris. He continued on, his eyes adjusting, when his boot scraped on something hard. He dropped to his knees with excitement, his hands furiously sweeping away the sand, and he cried out in triumph and relief at the asphalt below. But which road was it? Was it the road they had followed into the gorge that led back to civilization in the north, or was it the road they hadn't taken, a long barren trek to the port that had been their destination?

He kept sweeping forward on his hands and knees, and his shoulders slumped as he came to the edge of the pavement. This was the road that headed east to the port, and there was no way to know where he was on it in the dark sand-covered landscape. Was the road heading north to his east or to his west? He could walk ten paces to the left or right, and the road he sought could be there, but it could also be a mile in either direction or more.

There was just no way to know.

He pounded the ground with clenched fists, the frustration overwhelming. He could attempt to head east toward the port where there were people, but it was too far. He would never make it, though they would eventually find his body if he could keep on the road. Or he could head blindly north where civilization was closer, though still too far for him to make it. And worse, when he finally did collapse, he would be in the middle of nowhere, his body never to be found, his team forever entombed in the gorge he had foolishly led them into.

He stood and scanned the horizon for any signs of life, a Bedouin campfire, headlights, anything. But he found nothing. He sighed heavily, resigning himself to his fate, then turned east, toward certain death. He peered up at the stars, picking a new bearing. On the map, the road headed directly east and, assuming it was correct, if he could maintain his bearing and remain on it, his body should eventually be found.

He counted off a hundred paces, noting the entire time the ground felt firmer under his feet than it had before he had discovered the road. He stopped and kicked away at the sand once again, confirming he was still on pavement. He continued forward, gaining enough confidence to extend his hundred-pace intervals to two hundred as the ground beneath his feet continued to remain firm. He intentionally drifted to the left and right, immediately detecting when he was on unsupported sand, and smiled as his two-hundred pace check confirmed what he already knew. He was on the road, and as long as he paid attention, he would be fine.

He still had no hope of reaching the port, but he was confident he would eventually be found and, more importantly, his journal leading to his doomed team. His new confidence in not losing the road allowed his mind to wander, along with his eyes. With his vision adjusted and a half-moon overhead, he could see quite well, all things considered. He set a steady pace, though he was exhausted. He had enough water to carry him through to the end of the day tomorrow. His desert training had taught him that in situations like this he should travel at night and find shelter from the sun during the day.

What shelter?

He couldn't leave the road, though perhaps that wasn't necessarily true. The chances of anyone traveling it overnight after the storm were slim to none, and he was exhausted. He needed to rest. He scanned either side of the road, finding nothing, and was debating whether to simply lie down where he stood when something caught his eye—a sharp edge in the moonlight. He squinted. There was something definitely there, just to the north. If his eyes weren't playing tricks on him, he would swear it was part of a wall.

He struck out toward it, excited, and as he grew closer, any doubts he had disappeared. It was definitely a wall. The question was, what lay behind it? He reached the corner and extended his hand, patting the structure, his expert eye estimating by its construction technique to be from the New Kingdom, perhaps 2000 years old, likely one of the final things built before Egypt fell to the Romans with Cleopatra's death. He rounded the wall and gasped. Hints of several structures could be seen, whatever this was buried long ago in the sand, the storm from earlier likely revealing it for the first time in centuries, if not millennia. What was its purpose? Was it ceremonial? Was it a trading outpost? Was it military, or simply the home of some family long forgotten?

He spotted a structure, three of its walls exposed, and he walked over to it. It would be perfect. He dropped to his knees and began digging out the sand, revealing more of the wall on one side. He would sleep against it. It would provide him with some shelter from the chilly wind that continued to blow, though not with the ferocity of earlier.

He pushed aside the sand then paused, noticing an indentation that appeared to be expanding. He peered at it, confused, as what had begun as barely the size of his hand was now easily four times that.

What is that?

The indentation rapidly grew, not only in width, but depth, and he crawled backward, putting some distance between him and it. It reminded him of something. What, he couldn't be sure. Then he gasped as he recognized the pattern.

The sands of an hourglass as viewed from the top.

He leaped to his feet but it was too late. Whatever he was standing upon, that was anything but the desert floor, gave way beneath him and he cried out as he fell into an abyss, flailing at the nothingness surrounding him before he finally hit the bottom, screaming in agony as his leg snapped, then struggling for air as the sand from above continued to pour down on him, quickly burying him.

He sputtered for breath, fighting to remain above the sand, but it was useless, his broken leg preventing him from getting any useful leverage.

"Help!" he cried. "Help me!"

But his pleas were only answered by the echoes of his own voice reverberating down the shaft of what he now suspected was an ancient well. And as he coughed for breath, his head tilted back, desperate for those last few lungsful of air, he could have sworn his death rattle sounded like the cackling laughter of whoever had placed the curse on the final resting place of a man who was to never have been disturbed.

Imhotep.

University College London Dig Site
Lower Nubia, Egypt
Present Day

"No, it's nothing to worry about at all. There's no need to call the authorities, at least not yet."

"Are you sure?" asked a concerned Reading.

Laura smiled, wishing she could give one of her favorite people in the world a big hug. "I'm sure. He's wearing a Nazi armband, and from what we found on him, it looks like he died in the late 1930s. He'd be classified as an archaeological find, though we'll obviously have to arrange with the authorities to have him returned to Germany for proper burial. He probably has family out there somewhere."

"So, you haven't called anyone."

Laura chuckled. "Relax, Hugh. Nobody outside of this dig site knows what we found except for you three. So, unless you tell someone, we're perfectly safe."

James cut in. "Okay. Forget about the body. What's this about a journal?" The excitement in his voice was contagious.

"You're not going to believe this, but he was an archaeology professor. His name was Bernhardt Stoltz. He worked for the German Archaeological Institute and, as far as I can tell, he was on a dig just north of here, part of Hitler's relic-hunting program in search of magic powers to win the war. He kept a journal documenting his work. Apparently, his team made an incredible discovery."

"What?"

"If we're to believe what he wrote, the untouched tomb of Imhotep."

"Holy shit!" exclaimed James. "Are you sure?"

"I'm as sure as he was sure. The only evidence I have right now is his writings and sketches."

Reading's booming voice cut in. "This Imhotep character, I've heard the name. Was he a pharaoh or something?"

"No, he was an architect and a physician."

"And many other things," added James. "He was also the mummy in that movie with Brendan Fraser."

Reading grunted. "Lovely. You two have got me mixed up with cults, terrorists, organized crime, and now the undead."

Laura giggled. "I'm quite certain we don't have to worry about that."

"Let's hope you're right."

"Just in case we aren't," said James. "Remember to shoot out its knees and then you can easily outrun him."

"Sod off."

James roared with laughter and Laura ached, wishing she was there with them.

"Anything in that journal to indicate how he ended up at your dig?" asked her husband.

"As a matter of fact, yes. Apparently, they received orders to pack up everything they found and return it to Berlin, and they got caught in a sandstorm. The entire convoy was trapped in a gorge just south of here, and it's his belief they were buried alive. He left to seek help before it was too late. That was the last entry. I guess he died trying to reach help."

"Did he give any indication where this gorge is?"

Laura smiled as she stared at the map laid out on the table in front of her. "I've got a map with an X literally marking the spot."

"Awesome!" exclaimed James. "What's your plan?"

"It looks like it's just across the border in Sudan. Barely a kilometer or two in."

"One klick or a hundred klicks, it doesn't matter. You're going to need to get their permission," said Reading.

"I've already got Mary on it."

"I'm surprised she's still working for you."

Laura had been just as stunned to receive the call from the woman several weeks ago expressing her interest in continuing the job Laura's late brother had hired her to do. Laura had readily agreed, as the woman was an extremely effective travel agent and facilitator. The only difference between now and several months ago was that they now knew why she was so effective. "Yes, she called me a few weeks ago, said she was bored and had really enjoyed her job. James and I discussed it and we agreed having someone like her on our side had saved our behinds on several occasions—"

"Many occasions," interjected Reading.

Laura smiled. "Yes. Many occasions, and now that we know who she truly is and what she's capable of, we can ask even more of her."

"I hope you gave her a pay raise."

James laughed. "You'd blush if you knew how much we're paying her."

Reading groaned. "Don't tell me. My meager Interpol salary I'm sure pales in comparison."

"If you had her money, you'd burn yours."

"I didn't need to hear that."

"No, but you've been bitching every moment since you got on the ground, so I figured I'd give you just one more reason." James chuckled. "Your friend is flipping me the bird."

"He's your friend too," grinned Laura, dying to be there.

"Not when he's given me a one-finger salute."

Laura picked up the phone. "I'm going to let you go now. Now that we know there's no sense of urgency, I don't want you leaving until tomorrow morning."

"That's good, because I called Mo and he can't get us the RV early, so we won't be able to leave for two days regardless."

"That's fine. It'll give us time to explore more of the find, and maybe Mary can get the permits in place using her contacts."

Reading's voice grew louder as he no doubt leaned in toward James' phone. "And Laura?"

"Yes?"

"Don't go and do anything foolish now."

She giggled. "Who, me?"

The Nile Ritz-Carlton

Cairo, Egypt

Acton glanced at Reading as the call ended, his friend's face creased with concern. "What?"

"You do know who we were just talking to, don't you?"

Acton gave him a look. "Yes, and?"

"And she's as stupid as you are. If she gets that paperwork before we get there, she's going and you know it."

Acton sighed. His friend was right. Laura was exactly like him. It was one of the reasons he loved her so much, and why they far too often charged forward before weighing the risks. "You're probably right, but we can't get that RV any earlier than when we booked it for."

"Are you willing to wait two days?"

Acton chewed his cheek for a moment, weighing the alternatives. They could leave now in the Mercedes and arrive by nightfall, but Reading's health wasn't what it used to be, and he genuinely required the air-conditioned, comfortable RV. Even just a day or two in the oppressive heat could kill the man or, at a minimum, seriously push back his recovery from all he had been through in the past year. "Well, we need that RV," he finally said.

"My comfort doesn't outweigh Laura's life."

Reading was a proud man, and Acton didn't want to say it, but it appeared he would have to.

"Dad, you need the RV. There's no way you can take the heat, not in your condition."

Acton shouted a silent hallelujah at Spencer's voicing of the shared concern. "Spencer's right. Would you feel comfortable driving it?"

Reading shrugged. "When I was in the Army, they trained me to drive pretty much anything."

Spencer raised a finger. "I have my bus driver's license. Before I decided to become a copper, I thought it might be fun."

Acton regarded the young man. "What changed your mind?"

"Turns out I'm too much like my old man. I can't stand people."

Acton laughed and gave Reading's shoulder a punch. "A chip off the old block, huh?"

His friend grunted. "The Readings have never been known as people persons." His eyes narrowed. "People people?"

Acton eyed him. "What do I look like, Grammar Girl? I'm an archaeology major, not an English major. So then, that's the plan. You two will stay here, and I'll head out. You can join us in two days."

Reading frowned. "I don't like it, but I don't see that we have a choice."

Acton eyed him. "What's not to like?"

"Two irresponsible fools aren't necessarily better than one."

Throne Room of Pharaoh Djoser
Memphis, Old Kingdom
2648 BC

"Tell me, my child, does your heart belong to someone already?"

Imhotep cringed, coming to a halt just short of the entrance to his pharaoh's throne room. He craned his neck in an attempt to hear the response, but it was a mere murmur, though he caught enough to know it was a girl.

And she was young.

Pharaoh Djoser's appetites were legendary. Like most of his predecessors, he had a harem that gave him access to women and even men from around the kingdom, and to a variety of concubines from foreign lands—enough that anyone's appetite should be satisfied.

But Djoser also liked them young, far too young. Prepubescent girls should be off limits, even for a pharaoh, who answered to no one as he was a god among men.

Imhotep thought of his own daughter approaching the age that Djoser prized. In an attempt to protect her from his pharaoh's advances, he no longer brought her to the palace, making excuses for her absence when the rest of the family was in attendance. His wife and sons were safe from the man's lusts—even Djoser wouldn't covet the wife of one of his senior advisors. But the daughter? Most would consider it an honor to have their daughter bedded by the pharaoh, a living god, and it sickened him how some of his colleagues paraded their children in front of the man.

"You're very pretty. Has anyone ever told you that before?"

Another murmured response.

"I mean, besides your parents. Has a boy ever told you that, a man?"

"Does my brother count?"

Imhotep clutched at his chest as he struggled not to vomit at the voice of his sister, the youngest of nine siblings, and almost thirty years his junior. He gripped the hilt of his dagger, his knuckles turning white as he battled to control the rage that surged through him. The betrayal was unfathomable. Djoser was his pharaoh, his god, but he was also his friend.

Countless days and evenings had been spent together discussing life and things in general, their positions set aside as subjects that entertained and plagued men the world over were debated, and he counted those times among his most cherished memories. Djoser was a good man, a good ruler, and a good friend, except for this one flaw.

Imhotep released the grip on his dagger, noticing two pharaonic guards eying him, assessing if he were a threat. Did they know to whom their pharaoh's attentions were directed? If it were their younger sister, would they suffer the rage he felt, or would they, like so many others, think it was an honor for the living god to lust after their sibling?

He stretched his fingers, releasing the tension, then continued forward, clearing his throat as he entered the massive room, open on one side to a view of the Nile that nourished their flourishing kingdom. He forced a smile, battling once again the rage that threatened to consume him at the sight of his sister, ten years old this season, sitting in Djoser's lap.

His friend glanced up at him and smiled. "Imhotep, my friend. So glad you could join us. I was just getting to know your sister." Djoser bounced her on his knee and she giggled, breaking Imhotep's heart. She, like so many others, had already fallen under the man's spell, only she was too naïve, too innocent, to understand what that meant.

Aya spun toward him, her face lighting up. She hopped out of Djoser's lap and rushed toward him, hugging him hard around his legs. He picked her up and brushed the hair from her face.

"What are you doing here?"

"Looking for you."

Djoser laughed. "She arrived only a few moments ago, looking for you. When she said who she was, I was shocked. I don't think I've seen her since her birth."

Imhotep was surprised at the statement, though as he thought about it, Djoser was probably right. He had never consciously kept his sister away from the man, though perhaps subconsciously he had, instinctively

48

protecting her from the unforgivable vice that consumed the one man in the kingdom no one could say no to.

"Why are you looking for me?"

"Mother wanted me to remind you not to be late for dinner. It's Brother Ahmose's birthday."

Imhotep smiled at her innocent face and gave her a peck on the lips before putting her down. "I won't be late."

Djoser rose from his throne and approached, tousling Aya's hair. "Tell your mother that her pharaoh guarantees her eldest son will be home in time."

She beamed a smile up at the lech, then bolted from the room, Imhotep cringing at the sigh that escaped his master's mouth.

"What a beautiful young woman."

Imhotep gulped down the bile. "She just turned ten, sire. I would hardly call her a woman."

Djoser shrugged. "I see them all for what they will be and what they once were. To be there when they first blossom is one of the greatest joys in life. Do you not agree?"

Imhotep was at a loss as to what to say. His skin crawled with his pharaoh's words, especially with them being expressed so soon after his sister's departure, leaving no doubt as to whom he was referring. "I'm sure my pharaoh knows what's best."

Djoser laughed and smacked him on the back. "I can see the subject makes you uncomfortable." He sat on his throne. "Now, what is it you wanted to discuss?"

"Your tomb, sire. It is ready."

University College London Dig Site

Lower Nubia, Egypt

Present Day

Laura returned to the main tent after having made a long overdue trip to the loo and grabbing a bite to eat with most of the team in the mess tent. She zipped up the outer flap then unzipped the inner, the two-door system helping keep the air conditioning trapped inside, and was surprised to find one of the newest members of the dig, Rachel Connors, leaning over the map with her phone.

Laura frowned, anger flaring, but she drew a calming breath. "May I ask what you're doing?"

Rachel flinched, evidently not hearing her enter over the hum of the air conditioner. "Oh, sorry, Professor. I was just getting a head start on cataloging this for the website."

Laura frowned. "I thought I made it clear that no one outside of this dig should be made aware of what we discovered."

Rachel's cheeks flushed and her shoulders rolled inward. "I'm sorry, Professor. I wasn't going to post them, I just wanted to have them ready for when you did give permission."

Laura relaxed slightly. Past experience had tainted her into suspecting the worst of everyone, but even innocent mistakes had resulted in tragedy, and Rachel was new. Very new. She had arrived only three weeks ago, the daughter of a friend of a friend of an alumni at her former college, a favor called in that she was forced to deliver on. She had nothing against the girl, but it was already evident she would never have made the cut if it wasn't for her rich parents.

Yet she always believed in giving people a chance to let them discover their own potential, and she couldn't exactly punish the poor girl for merely getting a jumpstart on her work, the job of maintaining the site's social media assigned to her since she apparently had quite the following. Laura had decided getting young people excited about archaeology couldn't be a bad thing, and perhaps this so-called influencer could do some good.

"Well, just make sure none of that leaves your phone. If word gets out, this entire area could be swarming with amateur treasure hunters or worse."

"Worse?"

"Art thieves who wouldn't hesitate to kill us all to get their hands on the treasure documented in that journal."

Rachel paled slightly. "People would kill?"

"People kill if you knock on the wrong door. You don't think they'd kill for millions of dollars in gold and jewels?"

51

"I'll be more careful." Rachel rushed toward the door. "I'm going to get something to eat."

Laura smiled at her. "You do that."

Rachel left and Laura turned her attention to the table with the map laid out and the journal opened to one of the back pages. From what she had observed, it appeared Rachel had gone through every page, likely photographing them all, exactly what Laura would have tasked her with eventually.

I just pray it doesn't leak somehow.

She thought back to the last time information had accidentally leaked, photos automatically uploaded to a cloud account that wasn't secure. She glanced over at the Starlink system that gave them broadband Internet access. It was a godsend, but it could also mean trouble if it were abused, either intentionally or accidentally.

She sighed and headed for the door when she heard the outer zipper. And Rachel protesting.

"Ow, you're hurting me!"

Laura's eyes narrowed.

"You're lucky that's all I'm doing!" said Jenny, her voice uncharacteristically tinged with anger.

The inner flap opened and Mitchell stepped through followed by Jenny, dragging Rachel behind her, gripping the protesting girl by the upper arm.

"When my daddy hears about this, you'll be sorry!"

"You selfish little bitch! If you've compromised this dig site, your daddy will have to find the body first."

Laura stepped forward. "What the hell's going on here?"

Jenny shook the arm she still gripped. "I just caught this little shit posting a video online about our find!"

Laura's eyes shot wide. "Are you kidding me?" She had feared an accidental leak. It had never occurred to her that the leak would be intentional.

"She's lying. I didn't say anything about what we found. I just told people that we found something."

Jenny pulled out her phone and tapped at it for a moment before handing it over to Laura. "This brain-dead social media junkie has put up half a dozen posts about the discovery, promising huge news to her over one million followers, and then a few minutes ago posted photos of the map and the journal."

Laura gasped at the latest video posted only minutes ago.

"Hi gang! I told you we found something big out here in the desert. I still can't tell you what it is, but I've attached some photos to tease you with until I can. And shhh, don't forget, it's a secret!"

Laura flipped through the photos, one that included the entire map showing exactly where the convoy carrying the remains of Imhotep and the contents of his tomb was thought to be buried. She stared at the young woman in disbelief. "I can't believe you would do this! What were you thinking?"

"I didn't do anything! I never said Imhotep. I never said anything about the body, about the Nazis. Nothing."

Jenny growled, her face red. "Are you truly that stupid? Have you truly led such a sheltered life that you don't understand there are

53

consequences to your actions? You told over a million people, 'shhh, it's a secret.' You think they're going to keep that secret? Just because you don't understand what's in those photos, it doesn't mean someone else doesn't understand. The pages you posted, so careful not to have anything written on them, had hieroglyphics. Those hieroglyphics aren't just pretty drawings, you idiot. They're a written language, and there are people out there who understand that written language. And all over what you just posted to over a million people are the hieroglyphics for the name Imhotep. And then there's the damn map!" She tilted her head back and screamed in frustration. "This is so infuriating!"

Laura held up her hand, sharing in Jenny's fury. She wanted to beat the little shit to a pulp. But unfortunately, this social media-obsessed generation only cared about gaining followers, and she now understood why the girl was here, someone so out of place it had never made sense to her. The only explanation she had come up with previously was that it was the last desperate attempt of a father to secure a reasonable future for his child.

So many of this generation were obsessed with making a living without actually working, they couldn't fathom the fact they had tied their entire future to social media platforms that might not be there in a year. If TikTok were banned, those million followers and the income that came from it were instantly gone. If Twitter decided to put up a paywall, the vast majority of people would abandon it and most of your million followers were gone. This girl was here because she hoped she would be on the scene when something was discovered that she could post to her followers, who would then share and like her ditzy relaying of the discovery so she could grow her following.

The reason didn't matter. The damage was done. Now the question was how to mitigate it.

"Where's her phone?"

Mitchell handed it over and Laura held it out for Rachel. "Delete everything."

"What?"

"Delete everything. All the posts."

"I can't do that. Do you see how many times those things have been liked and shared?"

"Exactly." Laura took a deep breath. This girl reinforced the stereotype, a stereotype that had always frustrated her. She often felt it was unfair to label an entire generation for the actions of the noisy few, but in this case, it fit. "Every second we waste means someone else sees it, someone else likes it, someone else shares it, which means even more people see it. If the wrong people see it, we could all be in danger."

"Yeah, well, I don't believe that. You said that earlier, but I think you're exaggerating."

Jenny grabbed Rachel's arm again, wrenching her toward her. "You moron! You do realize that this dig site was attacked by terrorists a few years ago because of something we discovered here, don't you? Word got out then and people died. A lot of people died. And if people come here again with guns, I'll kill you myself!"

Laura shook the phone still in her hand. "Delete everything. Now!"

Rachel growled. "Fine." She took the phone and furiously worked it, Jenny monitoring her progress on her own phone.

Laura grabbed a radio off the table. "Cameron, can I see you in the main tent, please?"

The radio squawked a moment later with a reply from her head of security, former British Special Air Service Lieutenant Colonel Cameron Leather. "Be right there, ma'am."

She turned to Mitchell. "Gather everyone in the mess tent."

Leather entered, his eyes questioning the still-open flaps. "Is something wrong?" he asked as Mitchell left, immediately sensing the mood of the room.

"We have a breach. Someone posted on social media a photo of the map and photos from the journal that anyone in the know will realize is referring to Imhotep."

Leather cocked an eyebrow. "After everything you told them?"

Jenny scowled at Rachel. "Well, shit for brains here is more concerned with getting more followers than following instructions."

Leather frowned. "I've always said unfettered access to the Internet was a mistake."

Laura was about to respond when Jenny beat her to it. "It was never a problem until daddy's little girl was forced upon us. Everyone here understands the importance of security because they have a brain."

"Stop attacking me!" cried Rachel, her shoulders suddenly shaking as tears rolled down her cheeks. Unfortunately, Laura couldn't be certain if they were tears of remorse or simply because she was deleting content that might have gained her another million followers.

Jenny tapped at her phone and an exasperated sigh escaped. She held it up. "I just checked. The posts are everywhere. Just because she's deleting it from her social media feed, it only prevents her followers who haven't already seen it from seeing it. Unfortunately, it was shared several thousand times already. It's all over the place. This is out there and there's no stopping it."

Leather pursed his lips. "Is there anything that she's posted that says where we are?"

Rachel sniffed. "I never said anything more than that I was in Egypt."

"Your posts could have been geo-tagged."

"No. When you're a public figure like I am, you make sure you have all that disabled. Nobody can tell where those photos were taken."

Leather dismissed the assurance. "It doesn't matter. It doesn't take a rocket scientist to figure out where she is."

"But we haven't found anything other than the body of a Nazi in the bottom of a well."

"Nobody's going to care about that. It's that map and the location marked on it. I can guarantee you that if the wrong people figure this out, they're going to be heading directly there, and by the time you get there following the rules, it'll be picked clean."

Laura cursed. Leather was right. There was nothing here to steal. It was the destination marked on the map where untold millions could be buried.

Mitchell poked his head in the tent. "Everyone's gathered, Professor."

"All right, I'll be there in a few minutes."

Rachel held up her phone. "I've deleted everything I can think of."

Laura took the phone and stuffed it in her pocket. "You'll get it back at the airport."

"Airport?"

"You'll be leaving as soon as arrangements can be made."

"But that's not fair! I did nothing wrong!"

Laura growled. "The fact you still think that, is exactly why you can't remain here. You're a danger to yourself and everyone here, and you're too naïve to realize it."

Jenny smiled smugly. "I'd take a hammer to her phone."

The thought had occurred to Laura but she had dismissed it. "No, there might be something else we need to delete or post in her name." She turned to Mitchell. "You and Jenny join the others. I'll be there in a minute."

Jenny frowned and reluctantly left the tent with her husband.

Laura indicated Rachel. "What can we do with her?"

Leather regarded the young woman. "Unfortunately, the law doesn't allow us to actually do anything. We can't even confine her. However, the fact that she no longer has access to her phone means she's no longer a risk. The damage is done. Now we have to live with the consequences."

It was disappointing, but Leather was right. They couldn't arrest her, they couldn't hold her prisoner, and they couldn't banish her from the dig as she was Laura's responsibility until she put her on a plane. She turned to the girl with the room temperature IQ. "I would ask that you remain in your tent except for meals and to use the facilities, but I can't force you to. That being said, I'm about to go and tell the entire dig what you did and how you put their lives in danger. So, something tells me you'll want to keep out of sight regardless. You are barred from accessing our Internet on any device and from entering this tent. Now, get out of my sight."

"This is so unfair!" screamed Rachel, her fists clenched at her side. "All I did was make some harmless posts! You said not to tell anybody what we found and I didn't!"

Laura bit her tongue and flicked her wrist toward the door. Leather took Rachel by the arm and escorted her out before returning and zipping up the flaps, the tent noticeably warmer since they had been left open in the excitement.

"Ma'am, I should tell you, crossing into Sudan without permission could prove dangerous. Crossing with weapons could get us shot or worse."

Laura regarded him. "What makes you think we're heading into Sudan?"

Leather gave her a wry smile. "Oh, I don't know. Years of working for you?"

Imhotep Residence

Memphis, Old Kingdom

2648 BC

Imhotep stood out on their deck, staring at the Nile without seeing, lost in thought as the birthday celebrations continued behind him, Aya's giggles and squeals of glee as a game of tug of war was played nearby in the fading sun, both gladdening and torturing his heart.

It was quite evident Djoser had set his eyes on his young sister, and from the way he had spoken of her, evidently saw no problem with that. It sickened him, yet what was he to do? If he said anything, there was no telling how Djoser might react. He might laugh it off and, out of respect for their friendship, focus his interests elsewhere, or he might be offended, for most would consider it a great honor.

And perhaps it was an honor if there were any future in it. But Djoser quickly lost interest in his conquests. He enjoyed their innocence, but once taken away, he craved it anew, and his position allowed him to get away with it time and time again, because the parents of those he took advantage of believed the child was blessed for having been taken by a god.

Imhotep closed his eyes. He was exhausted. He had been working on his pharaoh's tomb for as long as he could remember, his unique design having won over the newly anointed pharaoh all those years ago. The step pyramid, as it had come to be called, was awe-inspiring. Djoser had grasped the vision despite the sketches on papyrus and the scale models disguising its true awesomeness. Now that it was complete, Imhotep had to admit it was more incredible than he could have possibly imagined. Tomorrow they would be traveling to the site that would be Djoser's final resting place when he finally left this existence and joined the other gods for eternity. The reveal was a day he had been looking forward to for years, a day now ruined over concern for his youngest sibling.

Someone approached from behind and he turned to see his mother smiling at him.

"Imhotep, my son, why aren't you inside with the others?"

He forced a smile. "I have a lot on my mind."

"Yes, tomorrow is a big day for you."

"A big day for all of us."

"True, but that's not what vexes you, is it?"

His mother knew him too well to bother lying, yet could she handle the truth? And if she could, would he be horrified by her reaction? Would she be among those who agreed it was an honor, or like him who believed it was an atrocity?

"No, it isn't, mother. However, it's something I cannot speak of. Not yet."

She pursed her lips as she regarded him, then sighed. "Very well. I learned long ago not to pry into your affairs. You are by far the most important member of this family. You alone are responsible for our station."

He smiled at her. "We were hardly peasants. Father was a great man."

She patted his cheek. "Your father was a good man. You are a great man. That mind of yours is a gift from the gods. There's no skill you cannot master. Healer of the sick, designer of the largest structures ever built. It's no wonder our pharaoh, our king, counts you not only as his most trusted advisor, but his closest of friends."

Imhotep's heart ached at her words. Just this morning they would have honored him, but now they cut him deeply, for how could a friend not only desire but actively pursue bedding his best friend's ten-year-old sister? He had to stop this before it went too far, before Djoser's obsession with Aya became insatiable. But how he could accomplish that without turning his family into peasants or worse, was beyond him.

Minsk, Belarus

Present Day

Arseny Utkin checked the logs, quickly reviewing the thousands of hits, searching for anything that might be of interest to their clients. He had created bots that would crawl the Internet and social media sites, searching for anything that might be of interest to a collector. Paintings, sculptures, ancient relics, anything that might have hit the black market, been discovered accidentally and was not yet secure, or where somebody didn't realize what they had and it could be purchased for a pittance of its true value.

Most days, he found little to nothing to bother following up on and, even when he did, it almost always turned out to be nothing. It was a painstaking process, and he was already looking into how he could use AI to streamline it. It wouldn't put him out of a job. It would just put him out of *this* job. He was too good a shot for Tankov to do without him.

The team leader, Alexie Tankov, former Spetsnaz, entered the room. "Anything?"

Utkin leaned back in his chair. "A lot of buzz about something in Egypt. Some influencer claims she has made some big discovery. I'm just about to check it out."

"Influencer?"

Utkin leaned forward and clicked on one of the links and frowned. "Interesting."

"What?"

"Looks like she's removed her posts."

Tankov cocked an eyebrow. "Really?"

"People remove posts for various reasons, the most common being they had posted something by mistake." He launched his social media crawler and quickly found copies of the shared posts, including one with a set of photos. And whistled. He tapped a couple of keys, sending the photos to the main display in the room. "Well, if that's not a treasure map, I don't know what is."

Tankov smiled. "X never marks the spot until it does. What's it supposed to be?"

"The other photos were sketches, mostly hieroglyphics." Utkin shrugged. "Do you read Ancient Egyptian?"

"Only the dirty words."

Utkin laughed, and for a moment wondered if archaeologists had ever discovered Egyptian porn. He snickered and Tankov eyed him.

"What?"

"Ra's raw-dogging rampage?"

Tankov rolled his eyes. "You're convinced every ancient culture had porn."

"Of course." He extracted some of the symbols and popped them into a piece of translation software, the Russian appearing a few moments later. "Well, this is interesting. It's pretty rough, but one part of it the software is pretty sure of."

"What's that?"

"This refers to the tomb of Imhotep."

Tankov's eyebrows shot up. "Imhotep? I know that name."

"So do I."

"Which means he must be important because I know nothing. And if he's important, it means he was rich, which means he was buried with a fortune. Where does that map point to?"

"Looks like northern Sudan."

"Tell the boys to get ready. I've got some calls to make."

Saqqārah, Old Kingdom
2648 BC

"Magnificent!"

Djoser's cry of excitement as the massive structure came into sight sent a chill of elation surging through Imhotep, and he momentarily forgot this morning's surprise horror—his pharaoh had extended an invitation to the entire family to attend the unveiling, and had insisted young Aya ride with them in his palanquin.

It had sickened him to watch Djoser dote upon his little sister. His king, his friend, had insisted she ride most of the way in his lap until she had finally squirmed her way loose and into her brother's arms, and he was terrified at what it might have been that scared her away. It was clear Djoser wasn't pleased, but he had laughed it off, and soon after his final resting place had come into view, all was forgotten.

The palanquin came to a halt at the foot of the entrance, the dozen men carrying the massive litter lowering them gently to the ground, having carried them from the palace. An honor guard was in place, drums, trumpets, and a choir of priests greeting the pharaoh as he leaped to the ground. The guard snapped to attention and Imhotep stepped down, protectively carrying his sister in his arms.

Her mouth was agape. "Brother, did you build this?"

He laughed. "I designed it. Thousands upon thousands built it."

Djoser spun toward him, his eyes wide, his cheeks flushed. "You were right, my friend, to keep this from me, to insist I never visit the construction site. To be deprived of this moment would have been the loss of an opportunity of a lifetime. It's incredible! You have outdone yourself, my friend. The name Imhotep will go down in history, never to be forgotten."

Imhotep handed his sister over to their mother, then bowed. "You honor me with your words, my pharaoh, but this is a monument to you and your glorious leadership. Without your divine guidance, the kingdom could never have afforded such an undertaking, and this simple man's vision could never have been fulfilled." He shoved his fist in the air and shouted to the masses gathered, "All hail our king and god!"

Djoser smiled at him then extended his arms as the crowd roared. The two men embraced, a tremendous honor, and Imhotep couldn't help but be touched by the significance of his pharaoh sharing the focus of the festivities. As his family watched with pride, Djoser stepped back and turned to those gathered, holding up his hands, his arms outstretched above his head.

"Let it be known that your pharaoh is so impressed, that as soon as I return to the palace, I shall be commissioning a monument to the brilliance of my most trusted advisor and my closest friend, Imhotep!"

The crowd roared, and Imhotep's jaw dropped, his eyes bulging. For a mere mortal like himself to be honored in such a way was rare, and in time the honor bestowed by a god could lead to his own deification, an honor his descendants would enjoy for hundreds, perhaps even thousands of years.

It was overwhelming.

He bowed deeply. "You humble me, my king."

A gentle hand on his shoulder had him looking up to see Djoser smiling down at him. "And you humble me with your creation. Now, come, honor me further by describing what it is you've created here in your own words."

Imhotep stood. "Yes, of course." Unwarranted pride was frowned upon in the kingdom. However, this was something so monumental, no man nor god would deny him his due on this day. He extended an arm, slowly turning to bring attention to that which most had probably forgotten the moment they had caught sight of the pyramid. "A wide trench protects the entire complex, its breadth and depth a testament to just how much stone was quarried from these grounds to build what you see before you. A wall encircles the entire area, the height of six men. It has fifteen entrances, all but one are decoys designed to prevent those who have no business here from gaining access. This trench and these mighty walls will not only keep out those who would disturb your eternal slumber, but will also hold back the sands so that the grounds inside can be kept pristine by those tasked to maintain them."

Djoser's head bobbed in appreciation. "Impressive. I don't believe I've ever seen walls so high. They alone are worthy of high praise. Yet…"

He stabbed a finger repeatedly at the hero of the show, and Imhotep smiled, facing the massive structure, something he was quite certain was larger by far than anything ever constructed by man. "What inspired you? It's so…" Djoser searched for the right word but failed.

Imhotep held out a hand, inviting his pharaoh to lead the way, and his procession slowly approached the massive structure, everyone straining to hear its designer's words. Imhotep indicated the first level. "I know it's hard to imagine, but if you could ignore the five levels above the first, you would see it's much like many of our tombs to your predecessors. It is simply a mastaba, like so many others. But by adding five more on top, increasingly smaller in size, ascending toward the heavens, it represents our god on this earth and your ascension after your death. Which will hopefully be far in our future," he added as an aside, to which Djoser smiled and bowed.

"Let us hope the gods heed your words, as I am certain today you have their ear."

Imhotep returned the bow then continued. "This represents your ascension to be among the gods, and a sign to future generations that a great man rests here and should never be disturbed."

Djoser slowly shook his head in awe. "When you showed me the sketches and models so many years ago, I simply couldn't imagine this." He turned to the gathered crowd of dignitaries. "Let us all take a moment and appreciate the work of this great man, Imhotep."

Everyone faced the gleaming structure, the polished limestone stretching far into the sky, shimmering with the rays of sunlight beaming down upon it. It could be seen for miles even on a cloudy day, but when the sun shone down upon it, it glittered bright on the horizon and had already been drawing gawkers for years, proving the necessity of the trench and mighty walls that protected the complex.

Djoser gripped the back of Imhotep's neck, giving it a squeeze and a shake. "You have outdone yourself, my friend. This"—he sighed—"this is meant as a monument to me. However, I suspect that after scores of generations of our descendants have lived and died, the one who will truly be remembered is not the god who rests under this, but the man who designed and built it." He beamed at him. "And nothing would make me happier, for today, we are brothers."

The Nile Ritz-Carlton

Cairo, Egypt

Present Day

"Just to be clear, these are temporary work visas that will allow you to enter the country, check out the site visually, but not actually dig up anything. I'm still working on those permits, but they could take a few more days, maybe even weeks with the situation there. The only reason anyone is getting in is because there is nothing happening in the area and it's so short. I had to grease some palms just to get the visas for Laura and five of her students."

Acton and Reading exchanged looks. "Wait a minute," said Acton, who had delayed his departure after Mary had called to indicate the visas might be ready shortly. "Laura and five of her students? What about me?"

"Sorry, they'd only take people who were assigned to the dig. Your name's not actually on the list. You're there as a spouse. It's legal for you to participate as long as you're not paid."

"What about Cameron? Surely she's allowed some security."

"No, only academics. The Sudanese said they would meet her at the border and provide security to the site. Understand, this is a sunup to sundown permit. They'll meet her at the border, take her to the site, she can look around, then they take her back to the border."

Acton sighed. "Well, I guess it's better than nothing. When's this all going down?"

"Everything will be waiting for you to pick up at the Sudanese consulate in Cairo tomorrow morning."

"Sounds good. Let the Sudanese know we'll meet them at the border at 8:00 AM the day after tomorrow."

"Will do. And Jim?"

"Yes?"

"Tell her to be careful. I wouldn't trust the Sudanese as far as I could throw one of them, and that whole country isn't very secure. You've got rebel factions, tribal factions, and just plain thieves. Tell her to get in, get out, and then, if we do get the dig permits, to be prepared for a heavy security requirement and a lot of payoffs to the locals."

"Understood. It won't be the first time we've had to dip into the discretionary fund. Thanks, Mary. I'll keep you posted." He ended the call then turned to Reading, whose head hadn't stopped shaking through the entire conversation.

"This is foolish."

Acton regarded him. "Well, I wouldn't say foolish. It's certainly not a trip out to Walmart, but it's a sparsely populated area and she will have government approval and an armed government escort. It doesn't get much safer than that in these parts."

Reading grunted. "I just wish Cameron was going with her."

"So do I, but they would've never let him go armed."

"True, but his expert eye might be able to assess whether it's prudent to continue forward or beat a hasty retreat."

"Laura's had enough experience that hopefully she'll be able to spot any trouble in time. I realize it's not ideal and we both want to be going with her and the others, but that's not an option, and it's better than the alternative."

Reading eyed him. "Which is?"

"She goes in tomorrow alone without permission, without an escort."

Reading groaned as he sagged back in his chair. "You're right. Sometimes that woman has more balls than brains. She's worse than you."

He grinned. "Why do you think I married her?"

Imhotep Residence

Memphis, Old Kingdom

2648 BC

Imhotep sat absentmindedly picking at his meal, his appetite still not having returned after the festivities of two days ago. After the tour had finished, they had returned to the palace where Djoser had surprised him with a party in his honor, the likes of which no mortal had likely ever been thrown. It had been an exhilarating experience, but his concerns had ruined the evening for him, though he had hidden it well.

"What troubles you, my husband?"

He glanced at his wife sitting across from him at the small table, the homes of the rich and powerful quite similar to those of the poor when it came to dining, the only difference being the higher the station, the higher the chairs and table, though never high enough to approach the throne of a pharaoh. It was a small difference he was grateful for, as working among stone for decades had his knees in a constant state of protest. Peasants either squatted when they ate, or sat on chairs so low, that their knees couldn't bend any further should the chair be removed.

He frowned at his wife. He couldn't tell her the truth. He couldn't tell her that at the party, his friend, his king, his god, had once again focused his attention on his youngest sister. If only she were just a few years older, then it indeed would be an honor. Djoser was a good man if it weren't for this one vice, and should he take his younger sister as one of his wives, it would be a tremendous honor for the family, and she would have a remarkable life, wanting for nothing. But he had little doubt that wasn't Djoser's intention. He wanted to add her to his harem, and he wanted to add her now rather than years from now when it would be more appropriate.

He lied. "I'm just wondering what my next project will be. I've been working for twenty years on the same thing day in and day out, so I know nothing else."

"I'm sure you'll find something." She smirked at him. "Or you could spend your days at home with your wife. I'm sure we could figure out something to do."

He laughed. "A temptation even our pharaoh would understand."

His wife pursed her lips for a moment before speaking. "I know he's your friend and he's our king, but I did not like the way he was with Aya."

Imhotep's stomach flipped and his chest tightened. "What?" He paused. "What do you mean?"

She eyed him. "Don't tell me you didn't notice. I saw you eying them all evening. Every time she giggled, it was like a dagger to your heart." She gasped. "That's what's been troubling you, isn't it?"

He sighed and leaned back, pushing his food away. "Yes." Relief swept through him at the admission, finally able to share his concerns with someone he trusted, someone who wouldn't repeat what he would say to anyone else, someone who wouldn't report him for his disloyalty.

"How long has this been going on?"

He gripped his forehead, closing his eyes. "Only a few days. Aya came to the palace looking for me. It was the first time Djoser had seen her in years, and she's of that age now." His voice faded.

"She is by no means of *that* age." His wife pushed her own food away and servants rushed forward, clearing the table. "Have you told your mother?"

"No. It would horrify her, and I'm not sure how she would react."

"I would hope she would react like any mother would and refuse to let him see her."

"If he were any other man, that would indeed be the solution. But Djoser isn't any other man. He's pharaoh, king, a god. If I spoke with him and angered him, or even offended him, it could mean the end of everything for our family."

"But I've heard the words from his own lips. He considers you his closest friend, his brother."

"Yes, he does. But in the years I've known him, there were others whom he said the same thing about that no longer walk this earth for having said or done the wrong thing. I serve as his closest friend at his pleasure and nothing more."

"Then what are you saying? Surely you don't propose to sacrifice your sister in order to maintain your station?"

He vehemently shook his head. "Of course not. What I'm saying is we need to be very careful here, and warning my mother of what is going on could trigger an extremely unfortunate response."

"Then what do you propose to do?"

He frowned, a solution eluding him. "I don't know. Once Djoser has his mind set on something, it's usually impossible to dissuade him."

His wife's finger tapped rapidly on the tabletop then abruptly froze in mid-air, her mouth opening slightly. "I have a thought."

"Oh?"

"What if she were spoken for?"

His eyes narrowed. "What do you mean?"

"Well, I thought nothing of it until just now, but our pharaoh isn't the only one whose eye was caught by your sister."

He leaned back and folded his arms as a pit formed in his stomach as yet another undesired suitor entered the mix. "Who?"

"Thutmose's boy. He's only two years her senior and he couldn't take his eyes off her during the entire ceremony."

He tapped his chin as he pictured the boy, though not from the ceremony, for he had been distracted enough not to have even noticed there were guests there. The boy wasn't important. It was the father, the family. Thutmose was *haty-a*, the mayor of Memphis, a very senior post within the kingdom, and was respected by Djoser. It was entirely within the realm of possibility that the two families would unite in a pre-arranged marriage. He was quite certain that if he proposed it to the young man's father, he would jump at the opportunity, especially with the triumph celebrated by their pharaoh just this week. His station was on the ascent, and Thutmose would likely be eager to take advantage of that.

He nodded. "I think it's a very good idea."

"Do you think your mother will agree?"

"Absolutely not. She and father let every one of us choose our mates. But once I tell her why, she'll have no choice but to agree. It's the only thing that might save Aya from a far worse fate."

Minsk, Belarus

Present Day

"There's no guarantee," said Tankov as he reviewed the research material. "From what we can tell, some college student at a dig site in southern Egypt was there when they found what looks like a journal and a map. There are some photos of several pages of the journal. Everything's in hieroglyphics, but it's quite clear that the journal is referring to the tomb of Imhotep, and there's a map here with a big X on it that indicates a spot in northern Sudan that we're assuming is a clue as to where the tomb is."

Sheik Khalid, one of Tankov's more wealthy clients and more importantly, a gambling man, chuckled. "I see why you called me first. You have no idea if there's anything actually there. This site could have been looted long ago. If it was found once, it could be found again. Hell, it could have been looted minutes after the map was marked."

Tankov dismissed the suggestion. "No, there's something else going on here. This is a fairly modern map, probably early to mid-20th century, and the names are all in German. Also, the X is just across the border into Sudan. Imhotep should have been buried much farther north."

"What can you tell me about this Imhotep? I've heard of him, of course, but other than his name and the fact he's credited with constructing the world's first step pyramid, I know nothing."

"There's not much to know. His name was found inscribed along with Pharaoh Djoser, whose tomb you just referred to, on the tomb itself, which is incredibly rare. Likely some sort of honor bestowed upon the man because of his accomplishments. It was over a thousand years later that he became deified and you started to see references to him in their writings as a great physician and architect, and basically, a master of everything he put his mind to. Nobody knows much about him. In fact, nobody knows when he or Djoser died. We're talking Third Dynasty here, early Old Kingdom. There were as many as thirty dynasties that followed, thousands of years for the truth to be lost.

"All we can assume is that because of the position he held and his accomplishments, and the fact his name was inscribed on the Djoser pyramid along with Djoser's name, a pharaoh, remember, a living god, we have to assume he was quite wealthy. And the Egyptian belief system was that death was merely a continuation of life in every way, just on a different plane of existence. So, they would be buried with everything they would need to have a good life. Just like now, back then that meant cold, hard cash—gold, jewels, artwork. And then, of course, there's the man himself. How good would the mummy of Imhotep look in your collection?"

"Pretty damn good, I can tell you." Khalid sighed. "Fine. I'll wire what you need to your account, plus your usual fee on anything I decide to keep. Plus, I take twenty-five percent of anything you sell that I don't want."

"Done."

"When are you heading in?"

"The plane is already loaded. We're just waiting on one piece of equipment that I've been assured will be here within an hour. We'll be in position sometime tomorrow."

"I still can't believe that anything will be there. Somebody has to have found it by now. If that map is German, then that means Nazi, which means it's been probably at least eighty years."

"Oh, I wouldn't be so sure about that. There's one thing I haven't mentioned yet."

"What's that?"

"I've been looking at satellite photos of the area and it's just sand."

"So?"

"So, according to the map, there were gorges in the area a century ago, and now there aren't. Think about it. If the Nazis did find something, they would've received orders to bring it back to Berlin. If they were transporting what they found, that could explain why they ended up where they are."

"They got lost?"

"I doubt that. This is a remarkably good map. If I had to hazard a guess, if I were trying to escape a sandstorm, I might take refuge in a gorge. And if that storm were bad enough, it could fill in that gorge."

81

"If that's the case, how did the map get out?"

"Somebody must have survived. Or, worst case scenario, you're right, somebody already found it, and when they did, they found this map and journal. Maybe they tossed it aside and this dig in Egypt found it a few days ago. A lot of questions to be answered, but no time to get them."

"Agreed. Get your team to Sudan and let me know what you find. If you actually deliver this time, it could be the biggest payday of your career."

The call ended and Tankov frowned as he recalled what happened when they thought they had discovered the Ark of the Covenant. There was no way in hell he was risking a repeat of that. This time, anyone who got in his way was automatically dead. No negotiating, no deals, no compromises. Failure wasn't an option.

There was a knock at the door and Utkin poked his head in. "I just got word. Suck-and-Blow is being loaded on the transport now."

Tankov smiled. "Then let's get going."

Throne Room of Pharaoh Djoser

Memphis, Old Kingdom

2648 BC

Imhotep had agonized over the situation for days. The genuine fear in his mother's eyes when he told her of what was going on was heartbreaking. She had readily agreed to his wife's plan, further proving he hadn't misinterpreted her horror at what Djoser had planned for the most innocent of her offspring.

"How do you think Pharaoh will react?" she had asked.

"He won't be pleased, I'm certain. However, it might be enough for him to turn his attentions elsewhere."

She gripped his hand. "What if Thutmose refuses?"

Imhotep dismissed the idea. "There's no way he'll refuse. It's too great an honor for his family to unite with ours."

And he had been right. He had immediately visited Thutmose's estate, proposing the future union, and the eagerness with which the offer had been accepted demonstrated how Thutmose and his wife understood the honor. Imhotep had felt horrible at the deception, for should Djoser choose to pursue Aya, he could decide that eliminating his competition was the only way to do so without the outward appearance of dishonor—it was one thing to bed a girl so young, it was an entirely different thing to do so with someone promised to another, god or not.

The offer had been accepted under the condition that the two children formally meet and the situation explained, with the understanding that should they change their minds, it would be allowed.

This, of course, had always been his plan. The entire arranged marriage was merely a delaying tactic. Within a few years, she would reach the age where Djoser would lose interest. He had added the proviso that the marriage couldn't take place before his sister's thirteenth year, another condition readily agreed to. If it worked, it would save his sister, and then if she so desired, the marriage could be called off.

It was brilliant, yet it all hinged on this moment.

The two families were gathered in the throne room for the announcement. Djoser sat on his throne, smiling down at them, though his eyes were focused on young Aya. "Now, what brings two of my most trusted advisors before me today, one with his youngest sibling, the other with his youngest son?"

Imhotep and Thutmose bowed deeply. It had been agreed that Imhotep would do the talking unless Thutmose were directly addressed. "We come before you with joyous news. With your blessing, of course, my family is pleased to announce that Aya, youngest daughter of Ptah and Khereduankh, is to be mated to Sokar, son of Thutmose and Monifa, when she is of age." He bowed deeply once again, his eyes staring at the polished floor. "We humbly beseech your blessing of this union, for with it we are certain it will be a bountiful one."

Silence met his request, and he glanced over at Thutmose, bent over beside him. His heart pounded and sweat trickled up his back to his neck, his angle so steep. Footfalls approached and he caught sight of Djoser's sandal-clad feet walking past him.

"Is this what you desire, little one?"

Imhotep gulped. He was well aware his young sister didn't fully comprehend what was going on, but she did seem to pick up on the excitement of the Thutmose family at the prospect, and was always eager to please her mother and older brother.

"I think so," she murmured, and Imhotep squeezed his eyes shut as he cringed.

"You think so? If you are to be mated to this boy and spend the rest of your lives together, you should know so, not just think so."

"I know so?"

"Is that a question or a statement?"

"I don't understand."

There was fear in her voice now, and Imhotep's fists clenched as his instincts to defend his little sister struggled to break through his self-control. Then something remarkable happened. There was movement behind him, and young Sokar spoke with remarkable bravery that left Imhotep convinced this young man might indeed turn out to be a worthy mate for his sister.

"My pharaoh, you are upsetting my future wife with your questioning. If you have concerns about my suitability as her future husband, I can assure you I will do everything within my power to not only take care of her, but to bring joy into her life as I have seen my father do with my mother."

Djoser sniffed hard, an action Imhotep recognized from their years together, executed when he was both surprised and displeased. Sokar had spoken out of turn, an offense that could mean his head if he were a man. Yet despite his wise words, he wasn't. He was still a boy.

Djoser exhaled slowly. "Comforting words, my boy. And if your father is any indication, you'll make a fine husband. My concern is what does your future mate want?" He laughed, stepping back in front of Imhotep. "Rise my friends."

Imhotep stood, confused, Thutmose following though not with as much certainty, likely doubting whether he was included in the term "friends."

"Sometimes it takes a boy to remind a man of his place." Djoser grabbed Imhotep by the shoulders, smiling broadly. "Of course, my brother, I bless this union! May it be fruitful and produce many nephews and nieces to bounce on your knee in your old age."

Imhotep smiled, grasping his friend and pharaoh's arms. "Your words fill my heart with joy, and with your blessing, I have no doubt all our futures will be filled with the laughter of children and the joy their innocence brings." He had inserted the word "innocence" intentionally, though he wasn't certain Djoser would pick up on its significance, and perhaps that was best.

Djoser released him then embraced Thutmose. Thutmose said something, though the words were lost on Imhotep as he turned to see his sister, her eyes red, her cheeks stained, with young Sokar standing beside her, a protective arm over her shoulders. It was an almost laughable scene. The boy who would stand up to a god in the name of a love he couldn't possibly feel or understand. But his words, likely heard elsewhere but repeated well when they were needed, might have just saved Aya, and for that he would be eternally grateful, no matter how uncertain the future union might be.

He smiled at his sister and she returned it. He held out his arms and she rushed toward him, her own outstretched, but to Imhotep's horror, Djoser stepped between them and scooped her up, rubbing his nose against hers, the intimate gesture between those who loved each other once again casting shadows over his sister's future.

He glanced over at Thutmose to find the man's mouth agape, obviously having caught the intimate exchange. Imhotep gave him a look and the jaw snapped shut. He subtly shook his head and forced the smile that had abandoned him to reappear, for this was supposed to be a joyous occasion, and Djoser couldn't be allowed to suspect that there was any deception in today's announcement.

It could mean the end of them all.

University College London Dig Site

Lower Nubia, Egypt

Present Day

Acton embraced Laura, leaning back and picking her feet up off the ground as he planted a kiss on her that had them both lost in the moment. Snickers around them from other members of the team cut through the fog of lust and he put her down. He grinned at her then stepped back, holding out his arms. "Who's next? Terrence?"

Everyone laughed, the young man's cheeks flushing.

"Well, if you're not going to, I am," said Jenny as she rushed forward. Acton laughed and grabbed her, picking her up and giving her a kiss on the cheek, causing Mitchell's cheeks to blush even more.

"Hugh sends his love," said Acton, returning his attention to the love of his life.

"How's he doing?"

"Not happy, I can tell you that. If it were up to him, he'd be here and not me." Acton pulled at his shirt, sweating the moment he stepped out of the air-conditioned rental he had driven here. "My God, I forgot how hot it was."

"Let's get in the tent. You're going to want to see what we found."

Acton's heart raced with excitement at the prospect of examining the remains and, more importantly, the map and journal. But he held up a thick manila envelope. "I've got the visas and a bunch of other documentation here. Now, I'm sure you're all eager to find out who is going."

The anticipation on the gathered crowd's faces was evident.

"Now, I didn't make these choices and neither did Laura. This was all done by someone else with an eye to getting not only approval from the Sudanese, but also with an eye to what would be the best mix should something go wrong. So, it was decided that three Brits, including Professor Palmer, and three Americans"—he held up a finger—"not including me, I'm just the doting husband here and apparently know nothing about archaeology, will make up the team. And if you're not on the list, don't be too disappointed. The team will be going in tomorrow morning and back by tomorrow evening. This is merely a cross the border, see if you can find a big X in the sand, then return, type of mission."

"Who's going, Professor?" asked Jenny, excitement in her voice.

"The three Brits are Professor Palmer and yes, as you would expect because they have the most experience, Terrence and Jenny."

"And the Americans?" asked Laura.

"Valdez, Cossio, and Johnson."

Carlos Valdez stepped forward. "It doesn't really feel right, Professor." He waved an arm at everyone gathered, mostly students from Laura's former college in London. "Most of them have been here a lot longer than us. They should be going."

"While I agree with you, from a pure fairness standpoint, it should be Laura and five of her students, but like I said, the second part of the decision on who would go has to do with what would happen should something go wrong. If we have British *and* American students in trouble, then that's two governments we can call upon for help, not just one."

"And that's another thing to keep in mind," said Laura. "This is purely voluntary. This could be dangerous, we don't know. We'll be on the other side of the border at most ten hours, probably less. We'll have an armed Sudanese military escort the entire time and the area is sparsely populated. If anyone doesn't want to go, that's perfectly understandable."

Valdez chewed his cheek. "If I don't want to go, does someone else get to go in my place, like maybe one of the London students?"

Acton chuckled. "Nice try. No, everything is issued in the specific names I mentioned. Like I said, we would've done this in a completely different way if it was up to us, but there was wheeling and dealing going on in the background that we weren't made aware of until the decisions were already final. Like Professor Palmer said, if you don't want to go, you don't have to go. There's no shame, no judgment."

Jenny took her husband's hand. "Well, I don't know about any of you, but I'm definitely going."

Mitchell shrugged. "As much as I'm ready to piss my pants right now, I guess that means I'm going."

Acton turned to Valdez. "How about you?"

"Oh, I'm going. I just want everybody to know, I don't feel good about it, but there's no way in hell I'm giving up the chance to see Imhotep if I'm being forced to."

Friendly laughter from the others had Cossio and Johnson readily agreeing. "Count us in," said Cossio, who then turned to the others. "Sorry, guys, I'm sure we'll all get to go next time."

Laura agreed. "Yes, and if there is a next time, it'll be a proper dig, and you'll be getting first dibs. We'll probably cycle you through so that we can operate both sites. But don't worry, if there's something to find, you're all going to get a chance to see it."

Acton handed the paperwork to Mitchell. "Secure this in the safe, would you?"

Mitchell took the envelope then Acton slapped his hands together. "Now, show me what you found."

Imhotep Residence
Memphis, Old Kingdom
2648 BC

"I should have known a union between our two families, yours of such a higher station, was simply too good to be true. But never would I have thought you would put my son in danger, my family in danger."

Imhotep, racked with guilt, couldn't look Thutmose in the eye, for every word the man spoke was the truth. Djoser had thrown a party celebrating the union, and to his disgust and that of Thutmose, the only two in attendance that understood what was going on, Djoser hadn't been able to keep his hands off Aya during the entire event.

Thutmose had approached him before the festivities had begun, and Imhotep had ordered his silence, promising to discuss everything the next day when they couldn't be overheard. Thutmose had appeared at the appointed hour and they now both sat, staring out at the Nile filled with boat traffic, the problems of fishermen and farmers trivial compared to what faced them now.

"I was desperate. This is all happening so quickly. It hasn't even been ten days since he met her, yet his intentions were clear from the moment I saw them together. You know how he is."

Thutmose eyed him, confused. "I don't understand. What do you mean 'how he is?'"

Imhotep sighed, closing his eyes and pinching the bridge of his nose. Perhaps it was a well-kept secret. Perhaps it was something only he was aware of because of how much time he spent with Djoser. Perhaps it was because he was one of the few that had access to the pharaoh's harem and saw the delights and horrors on offer. "I'm sorry. I thought people knew."

"Knew what?"

"About our pharaoh's...appetites."

"You mean this has happened before?"

"Then you've never seen our pharaoh's harem?"

"Of course not! He only grants access to family and visiting dignitaries." Thutmose's eyes bulged. "You mean you have access?" He sounded awestruck. All men of their station had their own harems, though they were typically merely a handful of women, most, if not all, local, sometimes one or two from the deserts to the west or east, or if one was truly lucky, a Nubian from the south. But the pharaoh's harem contained exotic treasures that had to be seen to be believed. It was the fantasy of every man in the kingdom to just get one night within its walls.

He refused to confirm his access. "What's important is that I am aware of pharaoh's, shall we say, questionable tastes, and I can't risk my youngest sister becoming his next victim."

"So, you approached me with this disingenuous offer, drawing my family and my son into this twisted affair." Thutmose sighed heavily. "What are we going to do? It's clear our pharaoh still has an interest in your sister, despite her being promised to my son."

Imhotep leaned back and ran a hand over his bare scalp, detecting a hint of stubble, his ritual shave skipped this morning, much to the surprise of the slave tasked with performing it. He just wasn't in the mood for the entirety of the morning ablutions. "I don't know. You don't know him like I do. Once he's set his mind on something, it's almost impossible to get him to change it."

"Perhaps he needs a diversion."

Imhotep's head bobbed slowly. "Yes, I've seen that work in the past, though only temporarily. Unfortunately, nothing short of a war or some sort of crisis that affected the entire kingdom, like a drought, would achieve our goal."

Thutmose shot to his feet and paced, pulling on his fingers, cracking the knuckles. "We must send them away, at least her."

"And where would we send them?"

"Somewhere out of sight, far enough that it's not a simple thing for him to visit or demand she be brought before him."

Imhotep shook his head. "And how would I explain this sudden departure? He would know."

"What if she were to die?"

Imhotep's jaw dropped. "Excuse me?"

Thutmose waved his hand, dismissing his shock. "Not really die, but what if the world were made to think she had died? Perhaps she's swept

94

away in the Nile, never to be seen again, then she's sent somewhere else to live out her life with a new name."

Imhotep squeezed his burning eyes shut. It was unthinkable to send his sister away forever. It was as good as killing her, though perhaps that was a selfish way of looking at things. Would a life living with strangers, never to see her family again, be any better than the fate she faced here? Depending on how he looked at it, he would have to say a thousand times yes, yet he couldn't imagine life without her. "We need help."

Thutmose grunted. "Only the gods can help us, and something tells me they won't get involved. Not when one of their own is the one in the wrong."

Imhotep's eyes widened as a thought occurred to him. He looked up at the still pacing Thutmose. "You're right, the gods won't help us, but I've always believed that the gods help those who help themselves, and faith may be the key." He rose, excited. "When we die, we are faced with the Negative Confession, thirty-six attestations we must recite, proving our worthiness."

"Yes, of course, every child knows this. What of it?" Thutmose paused then shook his head. "If you're thinking what I think you're thinking, those laws don't apply to pharaohs, only to mere mortals like ourselves."

"Yes, I'm aware of that." He stepped closer, poking the air with a finger. "We have our laws, but does a pharaoh have his own? You and I both know there have been some truly horrible pharaohs in our past. If you were a god, would you want them joining you for eternity, or would you have some way of condemning those you deemed unworthy from joining you in the afterlife, or at least the same afterlife that you were worthy enough to join?"

Thutmose stared at him, his head slowly shaking. "I don't know, but it would make sense, wouldn't it? There are so few gods, you would think they would be selective in who joined them. But if there is such a list of unforgivable sins, I've never heard of it, therefore it must be a secret known only to the gods."

Imhotep smiled slightly. "And perhaps to those who advise them in spiritual matters."

Approaching Sudanese Airspace

Present Day

Tankov finished inspecting his gear, zipping up his bags as the others did the same. They were a twelve-man team, fully armed, fully equipped, ready for any trouble. Their contacts within Sudan had assured them safe passage, including an escort. The only requirement was that they keep their weapons out of sight until they were in the countryside, and to try not to shoot first. Palms had been greased, percentages of cuts negotiated, and if all went well, everyone involved could be enjoying a massive payday before the end of the week.

Utkin picked his way through the cargo hold toward him, wagging a tablet. "You're going to switch teams and kiss me when you see what I've found."

Tankov gave him a look. "Not even if you had the surgery."

The team roared, insults flying as everyone took their seats and prepared for landing.

"You say that now, but I saw you eyeballing my ass when I had to dress as a woman in Dubai last year."

Tankov chuckled. "Just because your ass looks good in a miniskirt doesn't mean I want to kiss you." He jerked his chin toward the tablet. "What have you found?"

"I've been going through a database of historical maps. You know how this old map that marks the location has a route traced out on it that leads to the coast, but then they obviously took a detour and headed directly south into Sudan? Now, according to the old map, they were heading directly south and were supposed to take a left and head east to the coast, but instead, they continued south into what we presume was a gorge, possibly seeking shelter from a sandstorm. The only problem is none of the modern maps show a road there. And because whoever traced out this route used a thick-tipped pencil, probably a grease pencil, they obscured the road so there was no way to be sure if anything was actually there.

"I found a map from the 1920s and it shows a road heading directly south and ending in Khartoum." He brought up a modern map and zoomed in. "You can see this same road coming out of Khartoum and heading north, but instead of continuing directly north, it takes a jog to the east before resuming its route north, where it crosses the border and joins up with the road on the Egyptian side, heading east to the sea. This new road shows up about twenty years later. I think something happened to the original road, and after the war, they rebuilt it but had to take a detour."

Tankov smiled slightly. "Because the gorge the original had run through was filled with sand."

"Exactly. From what I could tell, these gorges aren't deep. Ten or twenty feet, but trying to empty one out after a storm would be more trouble than it's worth when you could just build a new road."

"Does that mean you've pinpointed the old road?"

"Yep. Turns out the original was built by the British, and you know how their engineers like to document everything. They've been putting their historical archives online." He brought up another image. "And lookee what I found."

Tankov peered at the document. "What am I looking at?"

"The original specs for the road, with very precise coordinates for multiple key points, including the entry and exit to one gorge." Utkin brought up another image, a satellite shot with two sets of coordinates indicated. He tapped the northernmost point. "X marks the spot."

Temple of the High Priest
Memphis, Old Kingdom
2648 BC

Imhotep shivered. He had, of course, been in temples before, even that meant for Djoser only, but he had never been inside the inner sanctum of the high priest, Neper, one of the few men he actually feared. He had requested the audience shortly after Thutmose had left, and it had been granted for later that evening.

And he was terrified.

Should a mere mortal kill him, yes, he would be removed from this plane of existence, and after swearing before the gods he hadn't violated any of the 36 unforgivable sins, and because he had led a good life, he would gain entrance to the joys of the afterlife. But the high priest and those like him had the power to condemn his soul after the fact, denying him entrance to that which awaited all who were worthy. And the moment he had crossed the threshold into this forbidden sanctum, he had regretted his decision. He shouldn't be here. His intentions were deceitful, and should the high priest figure this out, not only would his life as he knew it be over, but his soul could be condemned for eternity to a horrifying, hellish torment.

Footfalls cut his choices to only one.

He drew a breath as the high priest entered. The elderly man stood behind his desk and stared at him through sunken eyes. Imhotep's watered and his nostrils burned from the torches and candles providing the only light, and the incense, burning no doubt for some purpose other than providing a more fragrant environment for the holy man to enjoy.

"I was intrigued by your request to see me. In all my years, I don't believe we've ever been alone together."

Imhotep bowed deeply. "No, I have never had the honor."

"After the events of this week, I would suggest it is my honor to be in your presence. The monument built to our pharaoh is an impressive achievement."

"I am but a humble servant of the gods who've guided my hands and those of the thousands also involved."

High Priest Neper smiled slightly. "Well-spoken and no doubt true. Now, what is it that concerns you enough to seek my counsel?"

Sweat trickled down Imhotep's bare back, and though the encounter had been cordial so far, even pleasant, he wondered how long that would last. With what he wanted to know, he would have to approach the subject delicately. He drew a breath, holding it for a moment. "It's about the Negative Confession."

Neper cocked an eyebrow. "Oh? Have you done something where you think you might fail one of the declarations?"

101

Imhotep forced a chuckle. "I think like most, I always worry, though I'm not here about myself. I have a friend, shall we say, and I'm concerned that he will fail the challenge despite deserving eternal joy in the afterlife."

Neper sat, gesturing for Imhotep to do the same, the chairs tall, the priest's almost a throne. "If your friend cannot pass the Negative Confession, then he's not worthy of eternal joy."

Imhotep shifted in his chair, pursing his lips. The question that had to be asked could reveal too much, but he couldn't see any other choice. "Let me ask you another question then. Whom does the ritual apply to?"

"To all."

"Surely there are exceptions? I mean, if a baby dies at birth or shortly thereafter, surely he isn't subjected to the same standard?"

Neper raised a hand in acknowledgment. "Yes, there are exceptions, of course, including children who have not yet reached puberty among them, for they are the most innocent."

Imhotep seized on the statement. "Yes, those who have not yet reached manhood or womanhood are the most innocent, aren't they?"

Neper eyed him, and Imhotep feared the man had either figured out what this was about, or was beginning to have his suspicions.

"Are there any other exceptions? Those we would characterize as simple, who while their body may be that of a man or a woman, their mind is still that of a child?"

"They too are considered innocent."

"Any other exceptions?"

Neper shook his head.

"So, one's station doesn't exempt one from the challenges?"

"No, nor should it. The higher one's station, the greater the obligation to lead a good life in the service of others."

"So, no one, no matter how high their station, no matter how powerful, how wealthy, are exempt?"

"None."

Imhotep leaned forward. "None? Not even...one?"

Neper's eyes flared and he leaned back. "With the exception of our pharaoh, of course."

"Of course. After all, he is a god, and gods are not subject to the laws of man."

"No, they're not."

This was it. This was where he could pose his question without it appearing suspicious. "Are there any laws the gods are subject to?"

Neper folded his arms. "What do you mean?"

"Well, as we've been taught since we were children, there are good gods and bad. Surely in the afterlife, the gods can choose with whom they associate. They can't be forced to dine with those they despise."

Neper tilted his head forward, peering at Imhotep. "Are you asking if there are a set of challenges that even a pharaoh must pass to gain entry to the afterlife?"

Imhotep's heart hammered, his ears pounding. "Yes."

"Who are you to ask such a thing?"

There was no point in hiding it now, and admitting more of the truth might actually save him. "Because I'm his friend, and if our pharaoh's own words are to be believed, his best friend."

103

"And you concern yourself with the worthiness of a god?"

"I concern myself with the eternity that lies before my friend, who happens to be a god. There are certain challenges that we as mortals face that we both know he would fail, most of which are simply a fact of his position and are no fault of his own. I would assume any challenges that might face a pharaoh would exclude such things out of necessity. But are there others that even the gods consider unforgivable?"

Neper regarded him, a finger tapping his chin. Imhotep's stomach churned as the deafening silence grew. In life, this man had the power to not only have him put to death, but to condemn him for eternity. And Imhotep had little doubt the debate as to what his punishment should be now raged.

Neper finally broke the silence. "Like you, I am a mere mortal. Do the gods have their own challenges? That I cannot say, though I have no doubt they do. You are concerned about your friend, and despite its inappropriateness, you have sought my counsel over your concerns. This tells me that you are indeed worthy of the title 'best friend.' I suggest you return to your home and worry not over your friend, our pharaoh, for I can think of nothing he has done that the gods would consider unforgivable, that might deny him access to his exalted position in the afterlife."

Imhotep sighed heavily, his shoulders slumping. "I can think of one," he muttered.

"What was that?"

"Nothing." Imhotep rose. "Thank you. Your wise words have provided me with the peace of mind I so desperately needed."

Neper stood, eying him. "Yet I sense no peace whatsoever. Something still troubles you."

Imhotep scrambled for a plausible explanation, then again told a partial truth. "It's my youngest sister. She's been promised to Thutmose's son when she comes of age. I guess it weighs on my mind more than I realize."

Neper's mouth opened slightly, a smile spreading with the realization as to what was truly happening here. "I see." He rounded the desk, his eyes peering into Imhotep's soul. "There is deception here. You've lied to me."

Imhotep vehemently shook his head. "Not a word I have said has been a lie."

The elderly man continued to stare into his eyes, their noses almost touching now. "Your concern is over your sister, not your friend." Neper tilted his head slightly, peering at Imhotep from both sides, as if searching for a better view into his soul. "When I said that those of her age were the most innocent, you leaped upon those words, for that's exactly how you think of your sister, as innocent."

"Of course I do."

"And our pharaoh has been showing her an inordinate amount of attention these past days."

It wasn't a question. It was a statement. Imhotep kept his mouth shut rather than confirm his true concerns.

Neper stepped back abruptly. "I know everything. You, the concerned brother, noticed our pharaoh's attentions toward your innocent sister. Out of concern for her virtue, you arranged a wedding in the hopes our pharaoh, your best friend, would turn his attentions elsewhere, but as we both witnessed, it didn't deter him at all. Now you're trying to find something in the afterlife to save your sister, something you can tell our pharaoh that would scare him into stopping what he's doing."

Again, it wasn't a question, it was a statement, but it terrified him at how accurate the man's assessment was.

Neper frowned, shaking his head. "I'm afraid, my son, there's no comfort I can provide you, for the laws and moralities of man do not apply to a god. Ironically, the only thing that can save your sister from your best friend is his untimely entry into that afterlife you were hoping to use to influence his actions on this plane."

Imhotep stared blankly at the man for a moment, processing the words just spoken, then gasped. "You're not suggesting…" He stopped. He couldn't bring himself to say the words.

Neper smiled slightly. "Of course I'm not suggesting you kill our pharaoh. I was merely making an observation that should he continue to desire your sister, there's nothing you can do to stop it."

Imhotep dropped back into his chair, his head slumped, his shoulders rolled inward with defeat. "Then what can I do? I can't just sit by and let this happen."

"I've heard him call you his brother, not just his best friend. Have you considered that he might listen to you if you just asked him, friend to friend, brother to brother?"

"I already have in a roundabout way, and he seemed to miss my point."

Neper placed his hand on Imhotep's shoulder. "I have found in my dealings with our pharaoh that one must be direct. One must explain things in simple terms, for he thinks differently than we do."

Imhotep stared up at the man. "But if I confront him directly and anger him, the consequences…" He sighed. "I fear to even contemplate them."

"Oh, the consequences could be dire. It could mean your life, it could even mean eternal damnation of your soul should he order me to place a curse upon your body."

Imhotep gulped. "You would do such a thing?"

"I do as my god orders me to. The question you have to ask is whether your soul is worth risking in the hopes of saving your sister from her revolting fate."

Imhotep rose, sucking in a deep breath. "I would die for her."

Neper regarded him. "I have no doubt you would, but will you suffer eternal damnation for her?"

"Without hesitation."

"Then I think this matter is settled. Tomorrow, you must confront your friend, your pharaoh, and your god, and beg him to turn his attentions to someone else's equally innocent sister or daughter."

Imhotep's jaw dropped at the words, for none truer had ever been spoken. If he saved his sister, he would only be condemning another innocent.

There had to be another way.

Operations Center 2, CIA Headquarters

Langley, Virginia

Present Day

CIA Analyst Supervisor Chris Leroux pulled up the alert on his station located in the heart of the state-of-the-art operations center, buried beneath CIA Headquarters in Langley, Virginia. His team was prepping to support one of their operatives about to enter Belarus. He expected it to be fairly routine, but too often these days it seemed everything that could go wrong did go wrong.

His eyebrows shot up when he saw the alert related to Professor Laura Palmer, she and her husband James Acton two of the biggest pains in the asses he had ever encountered on the job, but they were also exceptional assets that had helped them out on many occasions, especially when they couldn't act officially.

The professors were owed.

He had set up alerts on the two of them, the computer monitoring for any mention of their names, and this time it had flagged temporary visas issued for Laura and five others, two Brits and three Americans, to enter Sudan for the day. He leaned back and folded his arms. One-day visas were unusual. Something out of the ordinary was going on, but there was nothing here to suggest any imminent danger. He turned toward his senior analyst and second-in-command, Sonya Tong.

"Sonya, can you run a check on Sudan? Has anything odd happened there in the past couple of days beyond the usual chaos?"

"Sure." She worked her station. "Why? What's up?"

"One of our favorite professors just got a one-day entry visa approved. Looks like she and five others, Americans and Brits, are entering and leaving Sudan tomorrow."

"One day? That's odd."

"That's what I was thinking, and it was just applied for and issued yesterday. That tells me whatever it is, is last minute. So, for some reason she urgently wants to get in there, see something, then get out."

The team's wunderkind, Randy Child, spun in his chair, staring at the ceiling. "How the hell did she manage to get a visa in one day to that country?"

"I'm guessing Mary's working for her again."

Child sighed. "Man, it must be nice to have money."

Leroux agreed. "Something we'll never have to worry about if we stay in these careers."

Child dropped his foot. "Speak for yourself. I expect my investments to pay off one day."

Leroux's eyebrows shot up. "You invest?"

"Heavily."

"In what?"

"Lottery tickets."

"The fool's tax!" cried one of their more seasoned analysts, Marc Therrien, seated in the back of the room.

"Somebody has to win every week," replied Child. "Might as well be me."

Therrien rolled his eyes. "No, somebody doesn't have to win every week. That's how the jackpots get so big. The odds of winning are so astronomical, you'd be better off taking all your ticket money and investing it in government bonds. In forty years when you're ready to retire, they'll be worth more than any winnings you might have got."

Child shrugged. "Where's the fun in that? I put ten bucks into lottery tickets and I can dream about winning it big until the day of the draw. I take that same ten bucks and put it in the bank, and what am I supposed to fantasize about? The six cents in interest I get at the end of the month? Sorry, I'll pay my stupid tax and have a little fun."

Tong interrupted the conversation. "This is interesting."

Everyone turned and she indicated the massive display arcing across the front of the room, footage of people boarding a massive Antonov AN-124 cargo aircraft shown.

"What am I looking at?" asked Leroux, standing, hands on his hips as he stared at the display.

"This is a few hours ago in Minsk. We've got an Antonov that filed a last-minute flight plan, final destination, Khartoum, Sudan."

Leroux scratched his chin. "Okay, you've got me interested. What's one of the world's largest transport aircraft doing going from Belarus to Sudan?"

"I'm not sure, but you're not going to believe who boarded it."

Half a dozen frame grabs appeared, faces isolated, and he didn't need to wait for the facial recognition software to tell him who he was looking at. Alexie Tankov, the head of a notorious group of art thieves, all former Russian Spetsnaz, a group they had had run-ins with before.

"Tankov? What the hell's he doing? Sudan's not exactly known for its art museums."

"I don't know," said Tong. "But if they're bringing this with them, then they're definitely up to something." She tapped her keyboard and an image of a large vehicle being loaded into the rear had Leroux even more puzzled.

"Did somebody call a plumber?"

University College London Dig Site

Lower Nubia, Egypt

Acton pored over the map while flipping through several others on a laptop. He glanced over his shoulder at Mitchell. "This is excellent work, Terrence."

"Thank you, Professor. Jenny helped, of course."

Jenny swatted her husband's arm. "Don't give credit where it isn't due. You bloody well know all I did was bring you water and massage your shoulders. This was all you."

Mitchell blushed and Acton chuckled. He tapped the coordinates indicated on the map. "This is good work, *whoever* did it." He turned to Laura. "If these coordinates are right, you won't even be three miles from the border. That should minimize travel time and maximize your time on site. What's your plan?"

"Well, we're not allowed to actually dig"—Laura indicated the safe with the paperwork—"but nobody said we couldn't use ground-penetrating radar."

Acton grinned. "Good thinking. The whole point here is to determine if there's something there. Hopefully, you'll pick up something and we can get in there with the proper equipment in the next few weeks."

"And if we don't find anything?" asked Mitchell.

"Then we don't give up. Ground-penetrating radar is extremely unprecise. It just detects disturbances underneath the ground, and it'll only do that accurately for so far, depending on the terrain. The information you found suggests that the gorge the road ran through wasn't very deep. What we're hoping is that we will spot something that justifies going back. But if we don't, it could just be that we surveyed the wrong area or that it's too deep and we need to excavate."

Laura tapped the journal. "This is too important to give up on. The contents of Imhotep's tomb are the find of a lifetime. I already lost Cleopatra. There's no way in hell I'm losing Imhotep."

Imhotep Residence

Memphis, Old Kingdom

2648 BC

Imhotep ground the pestle into the stone mortar, pulverizing the root into a fine powder to be used in a tincture that would soothe an ailing neighbor's stomach. He carefully poured the results of his efforts into a small wood flask then sealed it. He called for his eldest son, who rushed into the room, breathless, a game underway outside with many children of all ages from the neighborhood participating.

"Yes, Father?"

Imhotep held up the flask. "Take this to our neighbor Mysis. Tell him to take it with his tea. It should settle his stomach."

"Yes, Father."

His son took the flask and rushed from the room, once again leaving Imhotep alone with his troubled thoughts. The high priest's words had haunted him all night and day. For hours on end, he rehearsed what he might say, desperate to find the right combination of words that would persuade Djoser to leave his precious sister alone, and strike the delicate balance necessary not to offend the famously temperamental man.

Yet he could think of nothing that would guarantee the desired outcome. And even if he could find the words, it still meant condemning some other poor girl to a fate he found so revolting he was willing to risk eternal damnation. He washed the mortar and pestle to make certain the next preparation wouldn't be contaminated with today's efforts. While what he had prepared today was perfectly safe, if taken accidentally, there were many others that could have quite unpleasant, even dangerous side effects should they be accidentally ingested. He found cleaning up after himself after every preparation was the best way to make certain he never forgot. Inattentiveness in this profession, just as in construction, could lead to injury or death.

He stared at the opposite wall, scores of wooden boxes containing dried plants and flowers from throughout the kingdom and beyond, cured animal organs of all manner, elixirs with exotic names and questionable benefits. Within these walls, he could cure much of what ailed men, for he was a physician. In expert hands, what these boxes contained could just as easily kill. He sighed, facing a carving of Sekhmet, the god of medicine, her lioness head soothing.

What would you have me do?

His entire body shook, terror gripping him as a horrifying idea occurred to him, an idea so foreign, so revolting, it couldn't possibly be coming from his mind. He stared at the polished carving then shot out of his chair, sending it clattering across the floor as he slowly retreated toward the door, his mouth filling with bile at the solution that had just occurred to him, a solution so vile, so desperate, so effective, only a god could have conceived of such wickedness.

University College London Dig Site

Lower Nubia, Egypt

Present Day

Acton jerked awake, pushing up on his elbows to see what had woken him. He smiled at his wife as she double-checked her gear. "What time is it?"

"Time for you to get up."

He rolled off the air mattress, raised off the floor by a collapsible frame, and stretched, clawing at the sky overhead. He rose, noting a sense of urgency in Laura's actions. "Is something wrong?"

She grabbed her phone and tapped at it before handing it to him. "Read this. It arrived while we were sleeping."

Acton tensed when he saw it was from Chris Leroux, a friend of theirs from the CIA. It was a warning that a notorious group of relic thieves they had encountered in the past had landed in Sudan yesterday on last-minute flight plans. "This isn't good."

"No shit."

"You think the timing could be coincidental?"

"Hell, no. This is because that little shit posted exactly what I told her not to. They were obviously monitoring for anything out of the ordinary and found the map."

"What do you think the chances are that they have the actual coordinates?"

"Does it matter? We can't take the risk. Terrence used public records to find those coordinates, and that's all these guys do day in and day out. If we could find them, they could find them. And even if they didn't, that map provides them with the general area. At least we're going in with an armed military escort. That should hopefully keep things under control should they show up."

Acton took her by the shoulders, forcing her to face him. He stared directly into her eyes. "If they show up, you leave. Cede the territory. Just get your people, get in the car, and leave. No arguing, no nothing. Just get back on this side of the border and leave the find to them. We can try to fight it diplomatically after, but we've seen what they're capable of. They *will* kill you."

Laura opened her mouth to protest then sighed, snapping it shut. "You're right, of course. Everything will be fine." She put her hands on his and squeezed. "Don't worry, I'll be all right."

He gave her a reassuring smile. "I'm sure you will be." He doubted his words, but Tankov's team was in the capital and had a long drive ahead of them before they would get there. Laura was less than thirty minutes away, assuming the Sudanese escort was on time.

She checked her watch. "Time to make sure the others are up." She placed her hand on his cheek and gave him a kiss. "You're coming with me to the border?"

"Is the bear Catholic?" He grinned as he let go of her shoulders. "Does the Pope shit in the woods?"

"Leave the comedy to Niner, dear. He's better at it than you."

He recoiled in mock horror. "Them's fightin' words."

She giggled and unzipped the tent. "Don't take this the wrong way, but I wish he were here right now." She disappeared outside, leaving Acton to wish the same thing.

If Bravo Team were going with her, he wouldn't be worried at all.

En Route to University College London Dig Site

Lower Nubia, Egypt

Reading peered at the road ahead, thankful the sun was now rising. Spencer was driving, which was an odd feeling, but the lad had so far done an excellent job and had guided the massive RV through the chaos that was Cairo, something he wasn't certain he would have been able to do himself without messing up the paint job.

"We're making good time," observed Spencer.

Reading grunted in agreement. Leroux had somehow found out he was in Egypt and had forwarded him a copy of a warning he had sent to Laura about some Russian art thieves they had dealt with in the past with deadly consequences. He had paced in his hotel room, deciding what to do, then woke Spencer. They packed up everything to check out, but according to the front desk, no rental agencies were open in the middle of the night.

"Why don't you call that travel agent of theirs? Isn't that her specialty?"

His son was right. One phone call, returned within five minutes by Mary despite the hour, not only had a rental arranged, but it was their RV.

"I thought it wasn't available until tomorrow."

"You have to offer the right incentive."

He wasn't sure what incentive she might be referring to. Acton had already offered cash and it was declined, so he feared it might be a promise not to burn down the rental agency. Whatever it was, he didn't want to know. Whatever offer or threat had been made had them in the RV an hour later, long before the agency opened for the day, and heading for the dig.

They would have made better time in a normal-sized vehicle, though not much better. Excessive speeding as a foreigner in Egypt wasn't wise and wasn't safe either. It was a long trip regardless, and while they might get there an hour later than in an SUV, at least they would be there a day ahead of schedule.

"So, these guys are really dangerous?" asked Spencer.

"Extremely. They're former Spetsnaz. No morals, no rules. They won't hesitate to kill you if you get in their way."

"Spetsnaz? That's Russian Special Forces, isn't it?"

"Yes."

"You've had some run-ins with them before and you survived."

Reading gave him a look. "Obviously."

Spencer rolled his eyes. "You know what I mean. How did you manage it?"

"Usually with the help of friends. As good as Jim and Laura are, they're not that good, and not as well-equipped. And this time it's just Laura, five students, no weapons."

"What about the Sudanese escort?"

"Ha! I don't trust them at all. They'll either run away, or fall in behind whoever has the biggest wallet."

"Well, wouldn't that be Laura, from what you've told me?"

Reading frowned. "Let me rephrase. The biggest wallet on the scene."

He checked the navigation system and cursed. They were still three hours away, and if something were to go wrong, it would likely happen long before they arrived. But even if it didn't, there was precious little he could do to help. He was unarmed and too damn old to go up against seasoned Spetsnaz. He stared at the road ahead, nobody in front of them. "Let's pick things up a bit. Minutes could prove precious."

Imhotep Residence

Memphis, Old Kingdom

2648 BC

"Do you love me?"

Imhotep's wife stared at him, puzzled. "You have to ask?"

He chuckled. "No, I suppose I don't. We were a good match right from the beginning."

She took his hands, concern in her eyes. "Why are you speaking like this? What's wrong?" Her eyes narrowed. "What are you going to do?"

He ran a hand down her cheek. "Nothing you need to concern yourself with, but should something happen to me..."

She squeezed his hands. "You're scaring me."

"That's the last thing I want."

She gasped then stepped back involuntarily. "You're going to confront him about your sister, aren't you?"

He shook his head. "I've come to realize there is no reasoning with the man. The risk is too great. While he might abide by my wishes, it

123

would likely change our relationship forever. More likely, he'd ignore them and have me condemned, possibly along with our family, and he'd make my sister suffer a far worse fate than she now faces."

She fell into his arms, holding him tight, her shoulders racked with sobs. "What are you going to do?"

"It's better you don't know. If anyone should ask, we never had this conversation. I merely told you I was bringing our pharaoh a gift of our latest vintage and that was the last you saw of me."

He wrapped his arms around her, gripping her against him, and whispered in her ear. "Please forgive me for whatever happens. The gods gave me no choice."

En Route to Exploratory Site

Sudan

Present Day

Laura's adrenaline was pegged. Things were off to an inauspicious start. The Sudanese escort had been two hours late. They had arrived with three vehicles, two escorts in each, and they had demanded Laura and the others leave the Mercedes behind, which would have meant most of their equipment. Bribes were paid, and all six of them were still together with their supplies. Unfortunately, paying the bribes had shown the Sudanese that they had money and they had it on them. She had done everything out of sight with James, but their escort would be fully aware there was more available should they want it. She would worry about that later. That was par for the course when doing business in these types of countries.

Her bigger concern was the Russians. Leroux had sent an update a few minutes ago indicating their convoy had left hours ago and could reach the area in less than four hours. She didn't want to be there when

125

they arrived, but she also didn't want to leave before she had her answer. It meant there were precious few minutes available to waste over nonsensical things like what car to use.

Mitchell, sitting in the passenger seat, pointed ahead. "Looks like they're finally turning."

Laura had been watching the GPS programmed with the coordinates to the entrance of the gorge, looking for a road that cut west, so far spotting nothing. She gently applied the brakes then followed the lead escort onto what best could be described as a trail. The Mercedes handled the new terrain with ease as the old light utility vehicle in front of them struggled. Thankfully, they didn't have far to go, otherwise she feared their escort might give up.

"Less than two klicks," reported Mitchell.

Everybody leaned forward, peering ahead for any evidence to prove their theory. To their left, to the south, there were indeed rock outcroppings jutting above the sand, though it was the only evidence that the geological formations necessary for a gorge were indeed here.

"One klick."

She glanced at the GPS. They were close enough now that it was counting down 100 meters at a time. It hit zero and she honked her horn three times while bringing them to a stop. The escort ahead slammed on its brakes, skidding in the sand as the two behind slowed. She put the car in park then turned it off and stepped out, quickly joined by the others.

She waved to the man in charge of their escort, Captain Yassin, who thankfully spoke English. She forced a smile. No matter how she felt about him right now, their lives were in his hands. "These are the coordinates, Captain."

He looked about, stating the obvious. "I don't see anything."

"And we weren't expecting to. If it were visible, somebody would have found it long ago. The fact that we can't see anything is good. May we proceed?"

"Go ahead. Just try to hurry up. It's only going to get hotter."

"Yes, sir." Laura turned to the others. "All right, as discussed, stay hydrated. If you get too hot, get in the car and turn on the air conditioning. The keys are in it. Right now, let's unload the equipment and get the shelter set up. Terrence, you're with me. Let's make a quick survey of the area and see if we can spot anything obvious and pick a starting point for the radar."

Her team sprang into action as the Sudanese watched lazily, cigarettes already lit. She confirmed with the handheld GPS that they were indeed at the correct coordinates. The edge of a rock formation stretching east to west was barely fifty yards south of them. Just to their east was the road they had turned off that eventually joined up with the replacement road. All the research Mitchell had done suggested they were in the correct place.

They continued forward and she pointed at the rock formation, spotting some exposed stone that dropped sharply into the sand. "That has to be it." She turned back. "Jenny!"

Jenny looked up from setting up the shelter. "Yes, Professor?"

"As soon as you've done that, deploy the drone. I want to get a look over this ridge."

"Yes, Professor."

She continued with Mitchell and her shins advised her she was walking uphill ever so slightly, the optical illusion of the uniform color surrounding them disguising the fact there was a slope that led up to the exposed stone. She wouldn't be surprised if a hundred years ago there had been a cliff face here with deep gouges carved out of the stone by an ancient river. It was further evidence that they were in the right place. They reached the top of the slope and Laura took a knee, brushing away some of the sand around the stone outcropping that she surmised was the eastern side of the gorge they were searching for.

She peered back at the cluster of activity. "How much higher do you think we are compared to them?"

Mitchell turned. "Not as much as I thought we would be. It's so hard to tell when everything is one color."

Laura agreed. "Put a number on it."

He shrugged. "Five meters? Maybe fifteen feet, as the Yanks would say. I still can't believe they haven't converted to the metric system."

She chuckled. "Don't get me started. I'm living there now and I still find it difficult. It's like they fear change." She patted the sand under their feet. "But if we agree it's about fifteen feet high, then our ground-penetrating radar should be able to pick up something no problem."

A whirring sound overhead had them both looking up to see a drone hovering above them. Laura smiled as Jenny walked toward them, the shelter now set up, the three Americans unloading the ground-penetrating radar from the roof rack. "Send it back to the shelter and take an altitude reading, then bring it back right over my head and give me a second reading."

"Yes, Professor." The drone whipped back toward the others and Jenny turned as she guided it. It hovered over the others and she took a reading then guided it back to Laura's position, taking another, the purpose-built device capable of precise readings necessary for their line of work.

"What's the delta?"

"Five point two meters."

She smiled at Mitchell. "Not bad. You were only out by twenty centimeters."

He shrugged. "Nobody's perfect."

"Have you met my husband? He'll tell you otherwise."

Mitchell chuckled. "That's only because he *is* always right. Just ask him."

Laura snorted. "I dare you to use that line on him."

Mitchell's eyes bulged. "Are you kidding me? Professors have always intimidated me. You two are the only ones that actually terrify me."

Laura tossed her head back and laughed then pointed at the ground. "Have them start here. I'm going to phone James and give him a status update. I'm sure he's worrying himself sick."

Mitchell stared at her in horror. "You're not going to tell him what I said, are you?"

She shrugged and winked at Jenny. "I make no promises."

Operations Center 2, CIA Headquarters

Langley, Virginia

Leroux rose, smacking his hands together. "Good work, people. I love it when one goes by the books."

Tong beamed at him, having just confirmed their agent had reported in from Warsaw, having successfully completed his mission in Belarus, the authorities apparently completely unaware he had been there.

"All right, everybody, it's been a long night. Everyone go home, get some rack time. I don't want to see any of you until tomorrow morning."

Everyone began packing up their personal items and he returned to his station, bringing up the footage of the Russian team heading out earlier today from Khartoum. He hadn't had time to properly review it, and wanted to make certain there were no surprises they had missed.

"Aren't you leaving?" asked Tong, standing with her bag over her shoulder.

"I just want to go over that footage from Khartoum."

"I'll give you a hand."

"No, no. You go home."

She gave him a look. "The faster it's done, the faster all of us get home."

There was no arguing with her. She would stay here all day for him. He threw his hands up. "You're right."

She sat back down and Child, halfway to the door, stopped. "Wait a minute. I'm not going to let you two have all the fun. Besides, I've got nothing waiting for me at home besides video games and stale Cheetos." He returned to his desk and Danny Packman pulled out his phone, furiously typing on it then wagging it in the air.

"I just told Steve I'll be running a little late."

And as Leroux leaned back in disbelief, his entire team returned to their stations. Then he realized what he loved most about his job. It was his team. They were a family, all of them in this together.

He sighed. "All right. You guys chose to stick around, so don't blame me."

Therrien grunted from the back of the room as he dropped into his chair. "Don't worry, boss. I don't blame you. I blame the professors, it's always their fault."

Leroux chuckled. "Truer words were never spoken." He stood. "All right. Let's make this quick so we can all actually get out of here. I want to review that footage and compare it to the day before. I want to see everyone that came off that Antonov yesterday and then everyone who left this morning in that convoy. Let's make sure we've got a one-to-one match. I don't want any surprises. Sonya, you divvy up the work." He turned to Child. "Randy, I want you checking for phones that were in Minsk and are now in Sudan. See if we can track them back. We might get lucky and find out where these guys have been hiding."

"You got it."

Leroux pulled up the footage again as the others set to work, and did a quick headcount of his own. And frowned. They had confirmed twelve had been on the plane last night and they were all White. Today's departure of the small convoy now heading north consisted of twenty, if his preliminary count was correct. Some were Black, which made sense—whatever deal they had made would involve locals. His team was already isolating faces and doing the matches, but he was more concerned with the broader strokes. He ignored the locals and instead focused on the Russians, quickly confirming what he already feared. Twelve Russians arrived but only eight left this morning.

Where the hell are the other four?

Egypt/Sudan Border

Acton peered through the high-powered binoculars from the Egyptian side of the border. He was not a happy camper. His stress levels were at max-capacity. If it weren't for the Russians, he wouldn't be concerned, but it had already been an hour, and they were now less than four hours out. Laura's last report indicated they were in position, had picked a starting point, and were about to begin scanning. If they were lucky, they could have confirmation shortly that there was indeed something buried under the sand, and Laura could pack up their gear and get to safety then request that the Sudanese secure the site. The fact they weren't allowed to dig was actually a blessing. The first confirmation that there was something there should be enough, though he wasn't confident Laura would be satisfied.

He handed the binoculars to Reading, whom he was quite certain was even more concerned. His friend had arrived with his son only minutes ago, and Acton was thankful to have the experienced law enforcement officer with them. Reading pressed the glasses to his eyes, slowly scanning before he found his target. He growled and handed the binoculars to Leather. "You can't see a damn thing with these."

"It depends on what you're looking for. I'm just making sure they haven't been joined by anybody, and that nobody's approaching their position."

Reading frowned. "You're right, of course. It's just so frustrating being so close yet so far. If something goes wrong, there's nothing we can do to help."

Acton scanned the horizon at Leather's words. The man was right. They shouldn't be watching Laura's team, trying to figure out what they were doing. They should be keeping an eye out for uninvited guests. He spotted something to the southeast. What it was, he couldn't be certain. He squinted, shielding his eyes, but still couldn't make out what it was. There was something dark above the shimmering of the sand. It could be an optical illusion, it could be a car, it could be a Bedouin on camelback.

He held out his hand. "Glasses." Leather passed them over and Acton peered through the lenses, adjusting the focus before gasping. "Oh shit!"

Operations Center 2, CIA Headquarters
Langley, Virginia

Leroux's discovery was confirmed moments after he made it. Four of the Russians, including their leader, Tankov, weren't in the convoy.

"I've got them!" announced Packman. "They left the hotel thirty minutes earlier." Footage appeared on the main display showing the four men fully geared up, carrying duffle bags, climbing into two vehicles driven by military personnel.

"Track them. We need to know where they went." Leroux already had a sneaking suspicion as to what was going on, and if he were right, it wasn't good.

Tong manipulated satellite footage, coverage of the capital decent at the moment due to the fact the country was a mess, allowing her to easily track the errant Russians. The tagged vehicles were tracked by the computer with Tong filling in the gaps where coverage was lost, and within minutes they had a destination.

Wadi Seidna Air Base.

Leroux cursed as the Russians were greeted by a Sudanese senior officer before they all boarded a helicopter and lifted off. "Find that chopper." He checked the time code. It had left almost two hours ago.

"Connecting to AFRICOM now." Tong worked her magic and the screens updated to display a live feed from a US Africa Command AWACS aircraft monitoring the region. A few more keystrokes and mouse clicks had one of the hundreds of targets displayed turn to red.

"Is that our chopper?"

"Yes. This is live."

"Put up our coordinates."

Tong worked her terminal then looked up.

"Why am I not seeing it?"

Tong frowned. "Because the chopper's right on top of it."

"Do we have satellite coverage?"

She nodded and brought up a live shot, zooming in on Laura and her team, the chopper entering the frame from the south. He attacked his terminal, sending a warning message, but unfortunately, it was a warning arriving far too late.

Exploratory Site

Sudan

"What's that?" asked Jenny, cocking an ear.

Laura stood upright and her stomach knotted as she recognized the thundering clap of helicopter rotors. "Everybody back to the car now!" she ordered.

She was met by blank stares.

"I said, back to the car, now!"

Jenny pointed. "There it is!"

Everyone turned, spotting the helicopter coming in low from the south.

"Let's go! Let's go!" shouted Laura, scrambling down the slope toward their SUV, the rest of her team following. Their Sudanese escort took notice, cigarettes tossed, weapons ready, Captain Yassin emerging from the air-conditioned Mercedes.

"We've got to get out of here now!" she yelled at him.

He peered at the approaching helicopter and snapped an order to his men, their weapons lowering. The thunder of the chopper was almost on top of them now. If it were the Russians, there was no escaping, but if she could get underway with her team before they were confronted, they might just let them go.

"We have to go!" she shouted again, but Yassin tossed a finger toward the chopper. "It's one of ours."

Unfortunately, that meant little. She was already aware that the Russian convoy headed this way had a military escort. She reached the Mercedes just as the chopper passed overhead, banking hard as she jumped in. The engine was still running, and she put it in gear, grabbing the satellite phone off the passenger seat as Mitchell climbed in. She checked the rear rows, and as soon as the sixth member of her team climbed inside, she hit the gas, cranking the wheel hard to the right, the four-wheel drive chewing up the sand, spraying it toward their Sudanese escort.

The chopper landed just to their right and half a dozen men poured out, two in uniform, four in casual clothes with only body armor and weapons to distinguish themselves from regular civilians. Assault rifles were raised and aimed directly at them. She pressed harder on the accelerator when gunfire erupted, tearing apart the engine compartment, bringing them to an abrupt halt. The cabin filled with screams from those she was responsible for, terrified at the prospect of being slaughtered in the Sudanese desert. She turned off the steaming engine and raised her hands as they were rapidly surrounded. One of the four she assumed was part of the Russian team stepped forward and indicated for her to get out.

She handed the satphone to Mitchell, keeping it low. "Try to send a message to Jim."

"What do I say?"

"Just 911. Then hide the phone."

"Don't you mean 999?"

"He won't know what the hell that means."

She opened the door and stepped out, closing it behind her, raising her hands once again. The man lowered his weapon and removed his sunglasses, smiling at her.

"Professor Palmer, we meet again."

She frowned. "I'd like to say it was a pleasure." She shrugged. "But, well, given the circumstances..."

He laughed. "I always liked you and your husband. There are very few Americans and Brits that can make me laugh. So, where is your husband?" Tankov jerked his chin toward the Mercedes. "Is he in there with you?"

"No. He's safely in Egypt and already aware of what's going on."

"And just what do you think is going on?"

"You're here to steal what we found."

Tankov smirked. "So, it is here."

Laura silently cursed herself. Only minutes ago, they had confirmed there were indeed disturbances under the soil that were big enough to indicate a vehicle buried under the sand. She had repositioned the ground-penetrating radar deeper into the filled-in gorge to check for a second target when the helicopter had been first heard. This was her fault. If she had just done what she had agreed to with James and simply confirmed that there was something here, they would have been gone five minutes ago. "You obviously saw the map, otherwise you wouldn't be here."

"Yes, an appalling lapse in security on your part."

Laura shrugged. "I come from a society where we trust that our people do the right thing. Unfortunately, it means sometimes we're let down. If you saw the map, then you know the source and you know it wasn't intentional, it was just naiveté. What are your intentions?"

Tankov nodded toward the Sudanese escort that now mingled with those who had arrived on the chopper, a colonel now in charge. "As you can see, I'm here at the behest of the Sudanese government who hired my team to retrieve what might be on their territory."

"And sell it to the highest bidder?"

He chuckled. "Of course. What need could the Sudanese possibly have for museum pieces? They'll receive a commission on the sale, and at the end of the day, everybody's happy."

She spat. "Everybody? What should be going into a museum will instead be going into the hands of private collectors. And if you're not careful, you could destroy vital pieces of history from an era we know little about."

"Yes. Third Dynasty, Imhotep. Are you suggesting that his tomb is intact?"

"Not his tomb, but the contents of his tomb." She took a step forward. "Listen, this needs to be done properly. Let my students go and

I'll stay and supervise the excavation. If we do this properly, together, then nothing gets destroyed."

He eyed her for a moment then shook his head. "No, we don't have time for that. This country's unstable as it is, and you and your husband have friends that I have no desire to encounter again."

Her chest tightened. "Then what do you intend to do with us?"

"Professor, I intend to use you all as human shields."

Egypt/Sudan Border

Reading grabbed Acton by the shirt, putting an abrupt end to his plan to run across the desert to rescue his wife. "Just what the bloody hell do you think you're going to do besides get yourself killed?"

Acton cursed and relaxed slightly, the change in body language signaling that his friend could let go. The phone vibrated in his hand with a text message. He checked to see it was from Laura's satphone.

911.

He handed it over to Reading. "Should we respond?"

Reading showed it to Leather, who nodded. "Yes. Whoever sent this might get the reply, but more importantly, so will the Russians."

"Couldn't that just cause problems?" asked Spencer.

Leather shook his head. "No, I don't think so. They're professionals. It's important that they know that we know that they have our people and that we know who they are. It might just keep them alive."

"But wouldn't that just be warning them that there could be a rescue attempt?"

"Yes, but that's not necessarily a bad thing. They're in there to do a job, and my guess is that as soon as their convoy arrives, they're going in, getting the job done as fast as they can, then getting out. That's a Sudanese military helicopter that brought them in, so they're obviously here with the permission of the government. They'll get what they came for, leave, and probably leave our people behind. The best thing we can do right now is make sure they know we know, then get in touch with Leroux and let him know what's happened. Just make sure you don't tell them where we are."

Acton took the phone back and quickly typed a reply before hitting Send, then prayed they were doing the right thing.

Operations Center 2, CIA Headquarters

Langley, Virginia

Leroux grabbed his phone, entering the extension for his boss' office. "This is Leroux. Is the Chief in?"

"Yes, he is."

"Tell him I'm coming up to see him. Urgent matter."

"Will do, Chris."

Leroux hung up and headed for the door, turning to Tong. "Monitor everything. See if we can pull some faces off their Sudanese escorts. If we're lucky, this doesn't go very high up and all we need is for Washington to contact the right people and the Russian invitation is revoked. Oh, and put together an executive summary. You know the Chief is going to ask."

"I'm on it."

Leroux headed out the double doors, securing the operations center against any stray signals, then jogged to the elevators, thanking God his team had stuck around. He boarded the elevator, organizing his thoughts. This wasn't an authorized op, and if it weren't for previous instructions from his boss, National Clandestine Service Chief Leif Morrison, he would have been illegally using Agency resources.

But his instructions from the Chief were clear when it came to the professors—they were allowed to observe, then if action were necessary, permission had to be obtained, and right now, he needed that permission. His team was there on their own time, but they were still using Agency resources. He needed permission for the ops center to be assigned back to him before the next shift came in, authorization for overtime, and he wanted to commit additional assets, at the minimum a drone. The State Department needed to get involved because this was a hostage situation involving American and British citizens, and they might need a Special Forces team put on standby for a rescue mission.

One piece of good news was that with the current situation in Sudan, America had a hell of a lot of Special Forces in the area, including one team that would be eager to get involved given the opportunity.

The elevator doors opened and he rushed down the corridor toward a set of closed doors guarded by two well-armed security personnel, behind which were the offices of the bigwigs, including Director Morrison. The guards recognized him and remained relaxed as he rushed up to them. He held up his ID then pressed his palm on the scanner. It flashed green and he was let through. He entered Morrison's outer office and was waved in by his assistant. Leroux opened the door and found Morrison behind his desk, yawning. The man covered his mouth and indicated for Leroux to sit.

"Sorry about that, Chris. It's not that I expect you to bore me, but I pulled an all-nighter as well." He gestured at his laptop. "I just read your update. I thought the Belarus op was finished and you guys were standing down."

"We were, sir, but something came up."

"What?"

"Trouble in Sudan."

"That's not exactly news."

"No, but it is when it involves our favorite professors."

Morrison gripped his forehead, massaging his temples as he groaned. "What now?"

"From what we've been able to piece together, Professor Palmer's team discovered something at their dig in Egypt that suggested there might be an important find just south of the border in Sudan. They secured visas for her and five of her team."

"Including her husband?"

"No, because he's not officially on the team roster, apparently. It was a day pass with a military escort from the border to the site and back. While all this was happening, their discovery leaked and we found out that a Russian team of art thieves that we've encountered before—"

"The former Spetsnaz group?"

"Yes, sir. We last encountered them in Ethiopia. They landed in Khartoum last night, a dozen men with a lot of equipment. A convoy with a military escort left Khartoum this morning heading north, presumably toward where Palmer was heading. Palmer and her team arrived at the site a couple of hours ago. What we didn't realize at the time was that four of the Russians didn't go with the convoy. They instead boarded a helicopter that just arrived at the site."

"Military?"

"Yes, sir. Military helicopter with an escort on board. They've joined up with the Sudanese escort that was with Palmer, and everybody's been taken prisoner by the looks of it."

Morrison cursed. "How do you know all this?"

"I received an alert yesterday about the visa being issued, and then did a little digging during the downtime on the op. My entire team volunteered to stay on their own time, but now that this has escalated, I need permission to commit more resources as this now goes beyond observation."

Morrison held up a finger. "Wait, she's a Brit still, even though she's living here. Isn't her team all from London?"

"No, sir. There's a group from Acton's university there as well. In this particular case, we have three Brits and three Americans now being held by the Sudanese and these Russian…I don't know what we want to call them. Mercenaries?"

"As good a label as any. All right, what are you asking for?"

"An ops center, ideally the one we're already in, authorization for overtime for my people, a drone tasked to the area, and a spec ops team on standby in case a rescue is necessary. My guess is the left hand doesn't know what the right is doing here since both Palmer and the Russians had military escorts. Palms are obviously getting greased. My guess is Palmer is there legally and the Russians less so. It could be as simple as some calls being made to the Sudanese government, and this all gets straightened out."

"Has anybody been injured yet?"

"It appears one of the Russians shot out the engine of Palmer's SUV as they tried to escape, but at the moment, no, everyone is intact. That might not last long, though, if enough money is involved. "

"All right, permission granted for everything you need. I'll contact Washington and let them know what's going on, see how they want to get involved. Use one of our drones from one of our covert bases. What kind of contact have you had with the professors?"

"Minimal except to warn them of the Russian's arrival last night, and then of the inbound chopper. Unfortunately, we didn't discover it until it was on top of them."

"Where's Acton?"

"He's on the Egyptian side of the border with Interpol Agent Hugh Reading."

"What about their security team? Colonel Leather?"

"With four men fully armed, but if they cross that border, the Egyptians will likely revoke everybody's visa and shut down the dig. I'm sure they don't want to be seen as getting involved in what, for the moment, is a Sudanese affair. "

Morrison indicated the door. "Okay, go. Get me an executive summary plus everything you've got so far. Washington's going to want to know more than the broad strokes if they're going to send in a rescue team."

Leroux rose. "Yes, sir. Sonya is putting together the report as we speak."

"Excellent. And start rotating your team. They're already coming off a long shift. If this turns into a full-blown op, I don't want mistakes being made because people are drowsy."

"Yes, sir." Leroux headed for the elevators, firing a message to Tong, indicating for her to send the report to Morrison as soon as it was ready. His phone beeped a moment later.

Already done.

He smiled as he boarded the elevators. There was no way he would be able to do his job without her, and he thanked God she was fully recovered from the shooting that had almost taken her life. The world and his life would be poorer if she weren't in it.

Egypt/Sudan Border

Acton peered through the binoculars, unable to make out anything beyond the fact that no one had left the area. It was so frustrating. A single burst of gunfire had been heard shortly after the helicopter arrived, and the going theory was that warning shots had been fired, or perhaps the Mercedes had been disabled. It was equally possible though, that his wife or one of the members of her team had been shot as a warning to anyone else attempting escape.

An SUV pulled up and two of Leather's team stepped out, one holding up a case. "Is that it?" asked Leather.

"Yes, Colonel. I tested it. It's functioning. And I've already paired it to our comms gear."

"What's that?" asked Spencer.

"It's a relay," explained Leather. "Professor Palmer's last report indicated they were putting up a drone. If we're lucky, in all the excitement, it's still deployed. If we can get this relay close enough, we might be able to pick up the signal."

"How close?" asked Reading.

"Half a klick. If we're lucky, because everything's so flat, we might be able to pick it up a few hundred meters farther out."

"And how do you propose we get it there?" asked Reading.

"I'm going to walk it out there. As far as we know, the Sudanese and the Russians have no clue that we're standing here watching. They're going to be looking for vehicles approaching, and not from this direction."

Reading dismissed the idea. "Absolutely not. If you get caught, they'll shoot you, and they're liable to shoot the hostages. And as former SAS, if the Sudanese get a hold of you, there's no telling what kind of international incident could occur."

"Well, somebody has to do it."

"I'll do it."

Spencer stared at his father. "Are you daft? You're already sweating like a pig. There's no way you can cover that distance in this heat. And what if you have to run?" Spencer vehemently shook his head. "I'll go."

"Hell no!" exclaimed Acton. "There's only one logical choice and that's me. If I'm caught, it makes sense that I would've gone looking to see why communications have been lost. Plus, I'm a civilian. You're a British police officer, you are Interpol, and you're former SAS," said Acton, indicating each of the men. "Me, I'm nobody."

Reading regarded him. "You're not exactly nobody, and the Russians know who you are."

"Another reason for me to go. They know I'm her husband and they know we're rich. And people like that won't shoot a payday unless they absolutely have to. And besides, you're all assuming I'll get caught." He indicated his clothing, everything tan. The chances of them spotting me are pretty slim." He gestured at the case. "Now, show me how to set it up. The sooner we get it up and running, the better. Someone's going to eventually notice there's a drone floating unattended over their head."

Exploratory Site

Sudan

Laura watched as Tankov spoke nearby with the colonel that had come with him, and her escort, Captain Yassin. She couldn't hear what was being said, but the glances all appeared to be directed at her. They had had multiple run-ins with Tankov's team in the past, and he was well aware of who she was and how wealthy.

The conversation broke and Tankov approached with the colonel. He smiled. "Professor Palmer, you'll be happy to know that I've managed to save your life."

She eyed him. "Am I supposed to thank you for that?"

He shrugged. "Some would, but it would be out of character for you. In order to ensure your safety, two of Colonel Abdeen's men will be taking you to Khartoum. And when this matter is over, you'll be set free after paying a substantial, shall we say, fine, for your illegal activities on Sudanese soil."

"What illegal activities?"

"According to Captain Yassin, you had permission to make a visual scan. No digging allowed."

"We didn't do any digging. We only used ground-penetrating radar."

"Ah, but that's not entirely true, is it? The captain said he saw you standing on the ridge, scooping away sand from that rock formation."

"I would hardly call that digging."

"*You* might not, but the Sudanese government does. So, you violated the agreement and are subject to substantial fines. Your visas therefore were immediately revoked the moment you violated the agreement, and now you're all in the country illegally and are under arrest."

"Fine," said Laura, tense, her heart racing, though she refused to reveal the fear gripping her. Being taken to Khartoum to pay a fraudulent fine then being deported didn't bother her. The question was, why was she being separated from the others? That didn't fit if they were all charged with the same crime. "Why am I the only one being taken to Khartoum?"

"You're being secured for your safety since you're the only one capable of paying the fine." The word sounded as if it were surrounded by air quotes. "The rest will be here to assist us when our equipment arrives."

"So, slave labor?"

"If you find it necessary to put a label on it, I would call them unpaid advisors. You said you were concerned about preserving the integrity of what we find. Who better than five of your own?" Tankov turned toward the colonel. "She's all yours."

Colonel Abdeen nodded, snapping orders to two of his men who approached her. Laura turned to the others, Jenny sobbing. Laura reached out with both arms outstretched, and a group hug ensued. "Do everything you're told. Don't do anything stupid. Don't fight back. Don't argue with them. The key here is to stay alive and uninjured for as long as you can. Help is on the way. You have to trust that." She lowered her voice. "Make no mention about James and the others. And don't worry about me. I'll be fine."

Something pressed against her breast and she inhaled sharply at what she initially thought was someone feeling her up. One of the Americans, Valdez, was staring her directly in the eyes. She glanced down and spotted a small rock pick pressed against her chest. She reached up and took it, sliding it between her cleavage.

"Now, just remember what I said. Nobody do anything stupid." She smirked. "That's my territory."

One of the soldiers snapped at her in Arabic and she broke the hug, standing straight and glancing down to make sure the rock pick wasn't visible. "I'm ready," she said. Each grabbed her by an arm, the grip like iron, and she glared at them. "Is this the kind of treatment I can expect?" Tankov whispered something to Abdeen and more orders were barked. She was released immediately. "Thank you," she said to the colonel, who bowed his head slightly.

She climbed into the back of one of the army light utility vehicles, her guards sitting up front. They pulled away and she forced a smile at her sobbing students, holding each other for comfort.

Please, God, take care of them.

Operations Center 2, CIA Headquarters
Langley, Virginia

"Where do you think they're taking her?" asked Child, the youngest member of the team opting to take the first shift. Leroux had sent Tong along with half of his team to the sleeping quarters to grab four hours of rack time, then they would switch out. Team members from the backup ops center had taken their places, keeping the OC fully manned for what had just become a more difficult operation if the hostages were now being split up.

"I don't know," said Leroux, "but I'm guessing either to Khartoum or the nearest military base." He turned to Packman. "Check our scheduled satellite coverage for the area. Will we be able to keep an eye on her the entire time, or are we going to have gaps?"

"Give me a sec," replied Packman.

Therrien cleared his throat at the back of the room. "We've got some other action happening."

Leroux turned. "What's that?"

Therrien jerked his chin at the screen and Leroux turned to see the satellite footage zoomed out, a lone figure crossing the Egyptian border into Sudan. Leroux groaned, recognizing the clothing. "What the hell is he up to?"

Therrien zoomed in. "Not sure, but he's carrying something."

Child grunted. "Knowing him, probably an M4."

"No, it's some sort of case."

Leroux sighed. "All right, let's keep one eye on him and watch all our hostiles, just in case they notice him as well." He reached for his phone and dialed Acton's satellite phone. It was answered a moment later, the gruff voice of Interpol Agent Hugh Reading on the other end.

"Hello, Agent Reading. This is Chris Leroux."

"What can I do for you?"

"We're showing Professor Acton crossing the border, and would like to know what he's doing."

"The daft bastard is attempting to place a communications relay near the enemy position. We believe we still have a drone deployed overhead. We might be able to pick up the footage, perhaps even hear what's going on."

Leroux leaned back. If he was in Acton's position and it was his girlfriend held hostage, he would be desperate as well and might do the same thing if he didn't know better. "We have a drone deploying to the area. It'll be there shortly. It'll give us full coverage."

"But not audio, I would assume."

"No, not audio. But the only way your drone is going to provide any useful audio is if it's very close, and there's no way that won't get noticed.

Is there any way to call him back? He could be risking his life for nothing."

"Only if we shout to him."

Leroux dismissed the idea. "No, that'll just draw attention. It's best they're not aware of your position right now."

"Then it looks like there's no way to stop him."

"Unfortunately, it would appear so. Right now, we need you to stand down and let us handle things."

Reading grunted. "I'll pass on the recommendation, though I can't guarantee it will be followed. Not if it looks like Laura's in danger."

Leroux scratched the back of his neck. "Then I guess you're not aware that Laura's no longer at her previous location."

"What? Was she in that vehicle we saw leave?"

"Yes."

"Where are they going?"

"We don't know, but we're tracking them for the moment. We assume they're headed either for Khartoum or a military facility."

Reading cursed. "Are you guys mounting a rescue operation?"

"I'm awaiting word on what Washington's going to do. My guess is they'll try to do things through diplomatic channels at first before they send in a team."

"We both know there's no way to handle this diplomatically. Nobody has complete control of this country, and we know the Russians can't be trusted."

"You're preaching to the choir, Agent. Unfortunately, all I can do is make my recommendations then hope Washington takes them. Right now, my biggest concern is preventing an escalation that might result in the death of Professor Palmer's team members and the professor herself."

Packman cleared his throat behind him and Leroux turned. "We're losing coverage of her in five minutes. We won't pick it up for another twenty."

"What did he just say?" asked Reading, having picked up the report over Leroux's headset.

"We've just determined that we'll be losing satellite coverage of Professor Palmer's location in five minutes and we won't regain coverage for twenty minutes."

Packman brought up the map of the area showing Laura's current position and her projected route, along with an indicator of where they expected to lose contact then regain it if those holding her didn't change course unexpectedly.

"What are the chances they go somewhere unexpected in that window?"

"Not likely. And there's nothing within an hour of where they currently are, so we should be able to pick them up fairly quickly."

"Your drone, can you redeploy it?" asked Reading.

"I could, but I'm not going to. It's more important to monitor where five hostages are than one. I'll be requesting a second drone, but it'll take some time to get in place. For now, I suggest you hold your position, wait for Professor Acton to return, then head back to your dig site. There's nothing you can do from the Egyptian side of the border."

"Like I said, I'll pass on your recommendation, but I can't guarantee it'll be followed."

"Understood." Leroux ended the call and stared at the display showing Acton heading across the desert in a desperate attempt to find out what was happening to his wife and their students, and he prayed his famous gut was wrong this time, for he had a sense that everything was about to go terribly wrong.

Throne Room of Pharaoh Djoser

Memphis, Old Kingdom

2648 BC

"I have something rather disturbing to discuss that involves you."

Imhotep tensed at Djoser's words as a naked Nubian slave refilled their cups with beer brewed on Imhotep's estate. "Something disturbing that involves me? That sounds ominous."

Djoser took a long swig of his drink, sighing with satisfaction, toasting Imhotep with a raise of his cup. "You've outdone yourself once again. I don't know what it is your family does, but not even my brewery can produce anything of such fine quality time after time. What's your secret?"

Imhotep was more interested in what the disturbing matter was, though he was accustomed to his friend's short attention span. "It's a family secret, but I will reveal that my experience as a physician plays a part."

Djoser regarded him. "How could being able to heal someone possibly affect the taste of beer?"

"Precise measurements and quality control are necessary when preparing many of the concoctions I use in my practice. The same consistency is applied to our brewing process. Being so precise allows me to experiment as well."

Djoser sniffed his cup. "I detect something different. Have you been experimenting again?"

Sweat trickled down Imhotep's back. They were never supposed to get onto this topic of conversation. He had hoped Djoser wouldn't notice that there was something different about tonight's brew, but he had been caught. "As a matter of fact, I did add a little something extra, and judging from your reaction, it was a successful experiment."

Djoser took another swig. "Absolutely. What did you add?"

Imhotep forced a smile, wagging his finger. "Family—"

Djoser cut him off. "Secret. I know, I know. I could order you to tell me."

Imhotep grinned. "Where would be the fun in that?"

Djoser laughed, placing his cup on the table, the slave rushing over to refill it.

"This is the last of your guest's gift," she whispered.

"That's too bad." He smiled at Imhotep. "Next time bring more!"

"Double." Imhotep took a chance. "You said there's something you wanted to discuss?"

Djoser's eyes narrowed briefly. "Oh, yes, that's right, I've decided to have Thutmose's boy executed for his insolence. Since your sister is promised to him, I figured you were owed the courtesy of knowing."

Imhotep's jaw dropped, his eyes shooting wide. "But he's just a boy!"

"He's of age, and he should have known better than to challenge his pharaoh."

Imhotep's mind raced in a panic. This had nothing to do with the insolence of a young boy, and everything to do with his sister. In his attempt to save her by arranging a sham marriage, he had condemned an innocent boy to death. Just as the high priest had predicted, an innocent other than his sister would suffer in her place. There was no stopping Djoser when he wanted something, yet he had to be stopped, a decision he had already come to, though this unexpected information could change the timing of things.

Unless it was already too late.

"Have you already given the order?"

"No, I'll give it in the morning."

"And what of his family?"

Djoser shrugged. "The insolence was the boy's alone. Assuming the rest of the family remains respectful, I see no reason to harm them. Thutmose, of course, won't be able to remain in his position. I can't trust that he'll have my best interests at heart after this. He'll be allowed to keep his holdings, but he'll be placed in a position of lesser importance."

"Perhaps you'll be in a more forgiving mood in the morning."

Djoser regarded him. "You would allow such disrespect to be shown to your pharaoh?"

"He's just a boy trying to impress the girl promised to him and the adults in the room by defending her honor. I think it shows character, that when tempered with age and experience, could prove valuable to the kingdom." He forced a smirk, raising his cup. "And should word of your forgiving him spread, perhaps more names will be necessary on your tomb. Djoser the tolerant, Djoser the forgiving."

Djoser grunted. "I do like the sounds of those." He pursed his lips. "Perhaps I had been too harsh." He drained his cup, wiping his upper lip with the back of his hand. "I'll see how I feel about it in the morning." He rose and Imhotep leaped to his feet. "I grow tired. Call on me in the morning and I will inform you of my decision with respect to the boy."

Imhotep bowed. "As you wish."

Djoser returned inside, the dozen slaves attending them rushing after him, leaving only Imhotep and several guards. He stepped down to the water and tossed the contents of his cup into the Nile then stared up at the moon, begging the gods for forgiveness for what he must do, and for what he had already done.

Djoser had to die, and should all go to plan, the kingdom would be mourning the death of yet another pharaoh by the time the sun rose.

Enroute to Khartoum

Sudan

Present Day

Laura sat silently as her captors nattered back and forth in the front in Arabic, a language she spoke but had given them no indication she understood. She had a small rock pick that she could use as a weapon, but the question was should she use it? She might be able to take the two of them out, though it would be risky. She would certainly have the element of surprise, and that might be enough. But then what? Would she dump their bodies then commandeer the vehicle? And where would she go? She couldn't go back to the dig.

She smiled slightly. She didn't have to go back. All she had to do was get across the border back into Egypt.

The driver glanced in the rearview mirror. "What are you smiling about?" he asked in broken English.

"I'm not smiling. I'm grimacing."

"What does that mean, grimacing?"

English was obviously not this man's strong suit. "It's an expression you make when you're not happy."

He frowned but returned his attention to the road, switching back to Arabic. "I've always wanted a White woman."

His partner twisted in his seat, his eyes roaming Laura's body. "Me too. She's a little older than what I'm used to, but it looks like she still has an amazing body."

Laura's skin crawled but she didn't let on that she understood what they were saying. Instead, she began plotting her exact moves should it become necessary to defend herself. She would rather die than be raped, but she would prefer a third alternative. Hopefully, it was just talk and they wouldn't risk compromising their orders.

"If you're into it, we could stop up ahead and have some fun for a while," said the driver.

"Then we'd be late."

The driver shrugged. "So? We'll just say the engine overheated and we had to wait a couple of hours for it to cool down."

His partner grinned. "We could claim a lot of engine trouble and get there tomorrow."

The driver laughed. "I like the way you think, but tomorrow's too late. They'll all be dead by morning. Remember, the colonel wants no witnesses, no loose ends."

The passenger smirked. "Then we'd better find a place to pull over. I don't have any desire to screw a corpse."

Egypt/Sudan Border

Acton dropped to a knee and peered ahead as he unscrewed the cap to his canteen and took a swig, swishing the precious fluid around his parched mouth before swallowing. He could clearly see the dig ahead, and could make out the individual figures milling about, a cluster of five slightly to his left most likely the students. He searched for Laura but couldn't see her, though the shelter that had been set up earlier could be hiding her.

He had observed an army vehicle, one of the escorts that had led Laura and the team in, leave about fifteen minutes ago, but his eyes had been on the ground watching his footing, so he had missed who the passengers might be. He just prayed it wasn't Laura. If she had been separated from the group, he couldn't possibly see a positive way to look at that.

He slung his canteen and opened the case with the relay. He was still more than half a klick out, but there was a chance he might be close enough. Getting any nearer could prove dangerous. If he could see them, then they could see him. All it would take was for somebody to look in his direction.

The device indicated over a dozen signals, and the only possible source was directly ahead. He activated the relaying functionality which should clone all the signals and transmit them to the other piece of hardware in one of the dig's SUVs. The relay indicated its companion device was receiving the signal, and he breathed a relieved sigh.

He scooped sand around the case. It was matte black, but even that stood out in the uniformity of the desert. Satisfied he had hidden the case without compromising the signal, he lay prone on the sand and pulled out his cellphone, launching the drone app.

He found the signal and connected, the video feed appearing a moment later. He couldn't make out anything beyond sand, and his heart sank with the possibility the drone, in all the excitement, had been accidentally sent off and was nowhere near here.

He took a chance and slowly increased its altitude. He began to pick out details, some rocks, and he caught his breath as he spotted someone at the bottom of the frame. He continued to increase the altitude, careful to do so slowly so the engines didn't whine too loudly. More figures came into the frame and he angled the camera. It was a mix of Sudanese soldiers clustered near their two remaining vehicles.

He adjusted the angle and his heart raced at the sight of the Mercedes, its engine compartment blown apart. It didn't look like anyone was inside. He caught sight of the students grouped together, now sitting in the sand, terrified, though hadn't spotted Laura or the Russians. He adjusted the angle again to get a view of the shelter. He zoomed in. The four Russians were inside, talking with what appeared to be two Sudanese officers, but to his dismay, Laura wasn't with them, and there was nowhere else she could be.

Shots rang out and he flinched, looking up from his phone. Two Sudanese soldiers were shooting at the sky, and it took him a moment to realize they were firing at the drone. He dropped back down and sent it racing deeper into Sudanese territory rather than back to Egypt. He didn't want them knowing they were being watched from the border. The gunfire dwindled as the distance increased between the drone and the hostiles, and eventually stopped.

He looked up to see the Russians and the Sudanese officers were no longer in the shelter. It didn't appear any orders were being given to pursue the device, but his heart leaped into his throat when the four Russians fanned out, soon joined by the Sudanese, scanning their surroundings. Someone had obviously realized that there was a high likelihood the drone was controlled by somebody nearby.

He pressed as flat as he could into the sand, blind as to what was going on. He couldn't risk raising his head to look, but how long could he wait here? Would they send out a patrol to sweep the area, or would they wait him out? In a few hours, the rest of their team was arriving, eight more highly-trained Russians, plus God only knew how many Sudanese accompanying them. He had to make his escape before they arrived, he had to risk it.

He raised his head slightly, peering out from behind the mound of sand he had collected to hide the relay, then immediately dropped back down, spotting one of the Russians heading in his direction. This wasn't good. He was unarmed and, though trained, taking on a heavily-armed former Spetsnaz operator was too much even for him. He could try running, but he would be a sitting duck. There was no cover here in the desert, and he would be picked off if they didn't want to let him go. At a minimum, they would probably shoot him in the leg. His only option would be to surrender without a confrontation, then hopefully negotiate his way out.

The man's boots twisting on the loose sand had Acton holding his breath as he remained perfectly still. His only hope was that the Russian was focused far ahead of him rather than on the ground immediately in front of him. The footfalls continued to get louder and he exhaled, unable to hold his breath any longer. He gasped for air as quietly as he could when the Russian stopped. Acton couldn't be sure, but the man couldn't be more than ten feet from his position. He struggled to keep every muscle still, his unintentionally wise choice in clothing the only thing saving him now, unless the Russian was toying with him, standing there staring at him with amusement.

The man said something in Russian, and the only word Acton understood was "nyet." The footfalls resumed, and Acton breathed a sigh of relief as it was clear the man was returning to the dig site, having just reported his lack of success over some type of comms. He didn't dare make a sound, and had no clue what to do next now that his enemy was on the lookout for him.

Reading lowered the binoculars, handing them back to Leather as he let go a held breath, his heart hammering with what he had just witnessed.

The Russians were returning to the dig, Acton remaining undiscovered. The question now was what would his friend, what *could* his friend do? The Sudanese, all lounging about until this point, were now spread out in all directions surrounding the site, watching for any movement. There was no way Acton was going to escape undetected.

"Looks like he's stuck there for now," commented Leather. "If he waits until dark, he'll be able to walk out of there, but I don't know that he has that much time."

"Why not?" asked Spencer.

"That Russian convoy is going to be arriving soon. That's eight Spetsnaz plus additional Sudanese regulars. The first thing they'll do when they arrive is sweep the area far more thoroughly than what was just done."

Reading frowned. Leather was right. Acton had escaped detection only for the moment. "We have to warn him somehow."

Spencer peered over the shoulder of one of Leather's men holding a tablet showing the drone footage. "Looks like the drone's just hovering. How did he control it?"

"As soon as the relay picked up the signal then retransmitted it, his phone would be able to pick it up as well, so he probably has the app to control the drone on his phone, just from working at the dig site."

"Wait a minute. Are you saying that relay is sending us all the signals that it can detect?"

"Yes."

"And does that work both ways?"

"What do you mean?" asked Leather.

"I mean, is it just sending signals to us, or are we sending signals to it?"

"At the moment just to us. But it's capable of doing both. Why would you…" Leather's eyes shot wide and he smiled.

Reading stared at him. "What?"

Leather snapped his fingers at one of his men. "Switch it to bidirectional!"

"Yes, sir."

A toggle was flipped and Leather turned to Reading. "Do you think he was smart enough to put his phone on vibrate?"

Reading's eyes narrowed. "What do you mean?"

"I mean, if his phone is turned on, we can call him, text him, whatever, as if he was right beside you with a good cellular network."

Reading snatched his phone from his pocket then paused. "What if it isn't on vibrate?"

Spencer stared out at the desert. "Unless he's got the volume cranked, I doubt they'd hear it. And besides, what choice do we have? As soon as that convoy arrives, he's screwed anyway."

Reading hated to say it, but his son's assessment of the situation was right. He drew in a deep breath, holding it for a moment before he began typing, and said a silent prayer he wasn't about to get his friend killed.

En route to Khartoum

Sudan

The vehicle slowed and Laura's pulse pounded in her ears at what was to come. She breathed a sigh of relief when she spotted a group of Bedouins approaching on the road ahead. She stared out her window, unable to hide the fear she felt, and made eye contact with a woman walking with her two children. The woman stared back at her, her eyes flaring as if she recognized Laura's predicament, but the connection was broken as they continued past.

"Let's find a spot up ahead, off the road."

"You have no idea how ready I am for this."

The driver glanced at his partner's crotch and laughed. "I can see that."

This was it. This was about to happen. She had rehearsed what to do a hundred times over the past ten minutes, and she had to act fast. She reached under her shirt and slowly removed the rock pick, her head turned to the side, pretending to stare out the window, as if ignorant as to what was about to occur, all the while watching out of the corner of her eye to make certain her captors didn't notice what she was doing.

She managed to retrieve the small hammer and gripped it at her side. She ran her thumb over the metal, finding the head pointing away from her leg. She flipped it around so the narrower chisel tip was now pointing away from her.

The driver was focused on the road ahead, his foot heavy on the gas, the eagerness in his eyes reflected in the rearview mirror. The passenger pointed ahead. "Over there. You can park behind that dune. No one will see us and we can take our time." He began unbuttoning his shirt, no attention being paid to her.

If you're going to do this, you have to do it now.

She tightened her grip and slowly drew the hammer across her lap and to her left side, leaning over slowly toward the driver's side, increasing the distance between the beginning of her swing and where it would end so she would have a chance to build up momentum. She would only have one chance at this.

She drew a calming breath then swung as hard as she could at the passenger's head, tilted forward as he continued to undress. The tip embedded itself in his temple and he cried out as blood oozed. She didn't bother checking to see if the one blow was enough. Instead, she yanked the weapon free and swung again and again as the driver screamed for her to stop while he hammered on the brakes.

She adjusted her grip as she lunged forward, swinging again as the driver turned to face her. The tip punctured his eye and buried itself in the socket. He screamed in agony and lost control, the vehicle careening to the left before flipping on its right side. She slammed hard against the window but never let go of the hammer. She struggled to pull it free, but it was caught. She shoved the handle upward and the driver's eye socket broke with a sickening crack. She yanked the rock pick free, flipping it around and used the head to pound the man's skull repeatedly until it was clear there was no longer a need.

She confirmed they were both dead, then checked herself for any injuries sustained in the attack or the crash that might have gone unnoticed due to the excitement. She was fine, though her hands and forearms were covered in blood. She had succeeded in killing the men who would rape then murder her, but in the process had lost her only means of escape. The vehicle might still run, but there was no way she could tip it back over alone. She would have to hike it to the border, which was too far on foot.

Her instincts told her to get out as fast as possible and put as much distance as she could between the crash site and herself, but she calmed herself. She had time, and if she were to survive this, she had to think clearly. She climbed forward and retrieved all the water she could, then grabbed an AK-47 stuck in the footwell of the dead passenger, plus all the spare magazines she could find on both of them.

She repositioned herself, standing on the rear passenger window, pressed against the sand, then shoved open the rear driver's side door. She tossed the AK-47 out, along with the water and magazines, then struggled to extricate herself, battling the awkward situation and the bitch called gravity that kept trying to shut the door back on her.

She got her right foot up on the front passenger seat and pushed, finally getting her upper torso through the door. Escaping this beast was doing more harm to her than the fight for her life that had just occurred, but with each wiggle, each push, each pull, she gained another inch, and finally flopped over the side and unceremoniously dropped to the ground, the AK-47 adding a final insult by painfully digging into her ribs. She winced and rolled onto her knees, catching her breath. A throat cleared behind her and she nearly peed her pants.

Apparently, she hadn't escaped at all.

Egypt/Sudan Border

Acton flinched then put his Kegel exercises into practice so he didn't accidentally void his bladder. He fished his phone out from under him, thanking God he had put it on vibrate. How he was getting a signal, he had no idea, since he was in the middle of nowhere without a cell tower. Though as he told his students repeatedly, if you were ever in an emergency situation where communications were spotty, always send a text message rather than try to make a call, since a text message only needed a split second of connectivity to get a wealth of information out. His phone must have picked up a stray, and hopefully he could take advantage of it.

He kept his head down, careful to keep the phone behind the mound of sand that was his only cover. He couldn't risk the sun reflecting off the screen or the back-facing camera lenses—he would have four Russians on top of him in moments.

His eyebrows shot up to see a message from Reading.

Switch your phone to silent mode if you haven't already. We have connectivity through the relay. Are you secure?

Acton grinned at the device. It hadn't even occurred to him that it would relay his cellphone signal, and he certainly hadn't considered that it might be bidirectional. He quickly typed a reply.

Vibrate mode confirmed, secure for the moment, but I can't risk leaving my position without being spotted. Any ideas?

He confirmed he had no Internet connectivity. This was a purely cellular exchange, so the familiar pulsating dots he was accustomed to were absent. The message suddenly appeared in green.

Sit tight for now. We are going to try to figure something out.

He closed his eyes for a moment. He hadn't been expecting a solution to his problem, though his disappointment suggested he had hoped for one subconsciously.

Understood. I think they took Laura, can you confirm?

The reply confirmed what he already feared, but still broke his heart nonetheless.

Confirmed. She was taken in a vehicle by two Sudanese soldiers, destination unknown, though they're tracking her. Don't do anything stupid.

He sighed. What could he possibly do? He was helpless.

Imhotep Residence

Memphis, Old Kingdom

2648 BC

Imhotep sat in his chair, slowly sipping the boiled concoction meant to settle his stomach and counteract the root he had ground up and added to the batch of beer enjoyed earlier with his friend. He expected to be called upon at any moment, for by now, Djoser's stomach should be in such turmoil, he would be in miserable pain, retching out the contents.

He rubbed his own protesting stomach, thankful Djoser had called an end to the evening early so his suffering was only mild, as he had begun treating what was to come in time to avoid the truly horrendous effects of what he had dosed his friend with.

But was he a friend? Can one truly ever be a friend with a god, with a king, with someone who held your life in his hand, who could destroy you or even kill you, order you cursed in the afterlife for eternity should you offend him in some way? True friendship meant being able to say anything, to criticize when it was necessary. True friends fought, they disagreed.

In all the years he had known Djoser, they had never argued, never fought. They had their disagreements, but those were usually over trivial matters in the grand scheme of things. A true friend should be able to say, "Hey, hands off my sister." Though a true friend should never have to say it. The fact that Djoser saw no problem with this revealed he had no concept of what a friend was. And it meant his sister would never be safe until she was old enough to no longer interest the man, and that would be at least several years.

He eyed the small pouch sitting on his table, his heart pounding even faster than when he had created the preparation earlier in the evening. If he went through with this, he would fail the Negative Confession after his death and would be denied the joys of the afterlife, an afterlife meant to be spent with his family and friends.

He squeezed his eyes shut, the burn intense. He was doing the right thing. He had no choice. And perhaps the gods that would judge him would agree that saving the innocence of a child and countless more in the future outweighed his ability to state truthfully when challenged in the afterlife, "I have not killed." Yet he had no idea how the gods judged man. Was it always in absolutes, or was leeway granted as would be if men were to be his judges rather than deities?

There was a heavy rap at the door and he sucked in a deep breath as the house awoke. The rap repeated. The footfalls of a servant pounded toward the front entrance and words were exchanged, though he could barely make out what was said. He rose and headed for the entrance, finding one of Djoser's attendants in the doorway, his eyes wide, concern creasing his face.

"Oh, thank the gods! Sir, I bring urgent word from the palace. Our pharaoh is gravely ill. He asked for you to be brought immediately."

Imhotep feigned shock. "Give me one moment while I get my bag." He jogged back to his office and retrieved his medical kit filled with the various instruments of his trade and a common set of preparations that could cure or treat most ailments. He eyed the small pouch sitting on the table, and closed his eyes once again, the internal debate continuing to rage as it had all day. He pictured his little sister and sniffed hard, opening his eyes and grabbing it. He stuffed it in his bag and nearly ran headlong into his wife, standing in the doorway.

"What's happening?"

"Our pharaoh is ill and has asked for me."

She gasped and bit her knuckle as she stared at him, her eyes filled with fear. "Does this have something to do—"

He cut her off and instead leaned in and rubbed his nose against hers. "Never forget that I always loved you. And no matter what they say about me, remember I did it all for my sister."

His wife collapsed in his arms, sobbing. "Why have the gods cursed us? Why must you be forced to act when you've done nothing wrong?"

He held her tight, resisting the urge to join in her despair as he couldn't help but contemplate her question. Who was in the wrong? That was a question he had been asking himself since he had conceived of the plan, and all he could come up with was that either the gods had no concern about the lives of mere mortals, or there was no justice for gods—they were above all laws.

His heart leaped at a third possibility. Perhaps there *was* justice for gods, and he was their instrument of deliverance. Perhaps what he was about to do wasn't his idea at all but was instead given to him by the gods.

He squeezed his wife and pressed his lips against her forehead before gently pushing her away. He smiled at her. "Perhaps it is the will of the gods that guide me tonight. And should that be true, then we will see each other again."

He turned and headed for the entrance and his destiny, not believing a word he had just said to his wife, for what he was about to do had nothing to do with the gods, and everything to do with a man willing to sacrifice eternity for love.

Operations Center 2, CIA Headquarters

Langley, Virginia

Present Day

"We've got satellite coverage back," announced Child, working his station then jerking his chin toward the massive display.

Leroux rose, clasping his hands behind his back as he stared at the image. "Danny, left side, pull up footage of the hostage scene. Randy, right side, pull up her expected position."

The two executed their orders and a moment later a shot of the group appeared on the left. Leroux pointed. "Do a head count. Make sure everybody's where we expect them to be." He turned his attention to the separate feed on the right, showing an empty road. He glanced over his shoulder at Child. "Report."

He shrugged. "Well, it was just a guess."

"Get about ten klicks ahead of our max estimate then work your way back."

"Way ahead of you, boss," said Child as he continued to manipulate his station, staring at one of his screens. "Oh, shit."

Leroux tensed. "What is it?"

Child tapped his keyboard then indicated the display. Leroux's eyes shot wide and the entire operations center came to a brief halt as the image repositioned then zoomed in, revealing a vehicle lying on its side.

"See if we can get a tighter angle. We need to see if she's still inside that thing."

Child zoomed in but it was too steep an angle to see much inside. "The satellite's still too low on the horizon."

"Zoom in on the windshield." The image repositioned. Leroux pointed at the passenger's side of the window. "Zoom in on that and improve the contrast."

Child repositioned then the colors began shifting. Leroux peered at the image then spotted what he was searching for.

"Stop." He pointed, glancing back at the room. "What does that look like?"

Packman rose, leaning forward on his desk. "Blood spatter?"

Several others agreed.

"Somebody was definitely injured, at a minimum."

Child frowned. "Injured, sure, but killed? All three of them? You can't exactly go very fast on that road, but even if the driver lost control, they should have all survived."

"Maybe it just happened," suggested Packman. "They're still inside, injured."

"No, they're only a few klicks beyond where we lost visual. This happened maybe ten or fifteen minutes ago."

Leroux pursed his lips. "Zoom out again. Give me a shot where I can see directly around the vehicle."

Child complied, giving him a shot that appeared to be about twenty feet overhead, but still from a bad angle.

Leroux stepped closer to the display, scratching his chin. "If there were survivors and they got out, they obviously didn't go through the windshield because it's still intact, as are the driver's side windows."

"They would've had to have opened one of the doors," said Packman. "Then as soon as they were out, the door would close again."

"Exactly. Check the ground. Let's see if there are any footprints." The image changed, revealing sand with scores of indentations. It was difficult to tell what they were looking at from this angle, but whatever it was, it didn't look natural. Leroux sighed. "All right, when will it be high enough where we can get a shot through those side windows?"

"Ten minutes."

"Okay, we'll revisit this at that point. For now, have the computer searching for any movement, anything out of the ordinary in the area. If we assume this happened in the past fifteen minutes, then any survivors couldn't have gotten far. They could be lying in the desert bleeding out. Minutes could count here."

Packman asked the obvious question. "If we find her, who do we have that can save her?"

Egypt/Sudan Border

Acton continued to lay prone in the sand, the sun beating down on him. He checked his watch and frowned. The Russian convoy would be here within a couple of hours, then it would be too late. He would be found. He had to do something, because if he didn't get out of this sun soon, all they would find was a big-ass piece of crispy bacon wrapped in clothing.

His phone vibrated with a message from Reading, and a lump formed in his throat as he read it.

CIA reports Laura's vehicle in an accident. No visual on the occupants, including her.

He squeezed his eyes shut. The vehicle she was in was a piece of junk, possibly driven by an incompetent driver, and it was unlikely she would have her seatbelt on, if there was even one available. Yet even so, the speeds should have been relatively low. He couldn't possibly see all three of them dying, but they all certainly could have been injured.

He peered out from behind his cover. The hostiles were showing no indication they were aware of the accident. It could be hours before anyone came across the scene, and by then it could be too late if the injuries were serious. A rescue had to be mounted, and he could think of only two options. He could surrender then tell the Russians what had happened, and someone would be sent out to retrieve the injured, or he could go himself on foot. The road to Khartoum was barely a mile to the east. He could flag someone down and claim he had been in an accident, and they would take him to the scene.

Or you could call the Russians.

His eyebrows rose at the third possibility. He didn't have a phone number for them, but he did have the phone number for Laura's satellite phone, not to mention Terrence and Jenny Mitchell's cellphones. He cursed. What was the priority here? Saving Laura or evading capture? There was no question it was saving Laura, and unfortunately, his enemy had the best chance of accomplishing that goal. But as soon as they received that call, they might wonder how a cellphone was able to connect where there was no reception. As soon as they received the call, they might grow suspicious and send out patrols to see if he was close by, or worse, they could decide to cut their losses and run, possibly killing the students.

He wasn't too worried about the Russians killing the students. There was no reason. They were well aware that every police agency in the world knew who they were and had their faces. It was the Sudanese that terrified him. They wouldn't want witnesses to what they had done. If they thought they were being observed, they might execute Laura's team then leave, hoping there was no way for whoever was watching to identify them.

And they might just be right.

He growled, squeezing his eyes shut. Trying to save Laura could kill the others. And as much as he loved his wife, he also knew her, and her life for theirs was a trade-off she would never agree to. There was only one way she was getting saved. He replied to Reading's text.

Send me the exact coordinates.

Reading cursed and Spencer glanced at him. "What?"

Reading wagged his phone. "Jim wants the exact coordinates of Laura's crash site."

Leather cocked an eyebrow. "He's not thinking of going after her, is he?"

Reading regarded him. "Wouldn't you if it was your wife?"

Leather grunted. "If it was my wife, I'd call in an airstrike, but we're not married anymore. Now, my girlfriend, you're right, I'd do anything I could."

"What do we do?" asked Spencer. "He's going to get himself killed, and besides, how the hell's he going to get there on foot in time to make any difference?"

Reading regarded his son. "Sometimes it's not about succeeding. It's about knowing you did everything you possibly could, even if you failed."

Spencer's head slowly bobbed as he processed his father's words. "I guess you're right. So, we're sending him the coordinates?"

"I don't see that we have a choice."

"Then maybe we should create a diversion."

Acton pulled up the GPS coordinates and cursed. The accident had happened almost ten miles as the crow flies, and he wasn't a crow. But the distance to the ultimate destination wasn't what was important, it was how far he was from the road where he could hopefully get a ride to cover the remaining distance.

The phone confirmed he was less than a mile from that road, but a mile might as well be a marathon if he had to crawl on his belly the entire way, and it had him wondering what Reading meant when he said, wait for the diversion.

He readied himself then sent a reply.

I'm ready.

There was a shout, followed by gunfire. His instinct was to duck, but he instead pushed up on his elbows to find the Russians and the Sudanese aiming their weapons at the sky, all facing the opposite direction.

He scrambled to his feet then groaned, everything stiff from lying for so long in the heat. He forced himself forward, quickly picking up speed, then sprinted east toward the road, his head swinging back and forth, staring directly ahead then to his right, watching for any obstacles he might trip over, and making sure his enemy's focus was still on the opposite direction.

At least half a dozen weapons were firing at what he presumed was the drone, someone at Reading's end of things obviously having taken control. He kept running as hard as he could, more of his focus on his way ahead rather than his enemy behind him, when the gunfire dwindled then stopped. He dropped to the ground. He spun onto his back then

189

pushed up on his elbows, peering behind him to see the enemy's attention was still on the opposite direction. With the gunfire stopping, he had to assume they had managed to shoot down the drone, which meant there wouldn't be any more diversions. He scrambled to his feet and continued his push for the road, though at a crouch. The sun was high in the sky, brutal, baking the sand that surrounded him, waves of heat shimmering off the surface. He was far enough away now that anyone looking in his direction might mistake him for an optical illusion if he kept low enough.

His sprint during the shooting had allowed him to cover almost half the distance, but the remaining half would take far longer. He continued forward, his upper body, almost parallel with the ground, doing a number on his glutes. He wouldn't be able to keep this up for too long, and he questioned whether there was any benefit.

He took a knee, turning to face the enemy position, and smiled. There was no way they could see him, not from this distance, not with the heat waves obscuring the line of sight and the fact his clothes blended in with the sand around him.

He made a decision that he prayed didn't cost him his life, and stood, heading for the road, his muscles thanking him. He fished out his phone, careful to keep his torso between it and the Russians, then frowned. There was no signal. He was too far from the relay. It meant he was on his own, and with Sudan being what it was, it was unlikely he would be getting a signal anytime soon.

Operations Center 2, CIA Headquarters
Langley, Virginia

Leroux pointed at the display. "What's the cellphone coverage in that area?"

Child tapped at his keyboard and an overlay appeared showing coverage all along the road from Khartoum to the border. One of the circles had Acton's position within it, which meant they should be able to communicate with him. He reached for his headset when Child hit another key, the circles indicating coverage areas going gray.

Leroux glanced over his shoulder at him. "What are you trying to tell me?"

"That's supposed to be the coverage, but during the fighting, the network was taken down and they haven't had a chance to repair it. There's almost no coverage outside of the major cities right now."

Leroux cursed. "So then, we have no way to contact him."

"No, sir."

"I've got something!" exclaimed Packman, hammering his keyboard then pointing at the display. The satellite image showed a mix of people and camels.

"What are we looking at?"

"It's a group of, I don't know, Bedouins, maybe. They're traveling east of Palmer's crash site and they're close enough that it's conceivable she's joined them."

Leroux peered at the image. "I don't see anyone who's wearing Western clothing."

"Neither do I," agreed Packman. "But check this out." A few more keystrokes and a second image appeared. "This is from just before we lost coverage. Same group. The headcount is fifteen here." He jerked his chin toward the live image. "I'm counting sixteen in this group.

Leroux rose, excited. "So, they picked someone else up."

"It looks that way."

"All right, analyze the two images. See if you can figure out if it was a man or a woman. And if it was a woman, which one? We just might have found our missing professor. And let's see if we can figure out who these people are. Are they friend or foe? She may have just been rescued, or she may be on her way to her execution."

Egypt/Sudan Border

Reading's phone vibrated with a message from Leroux.

Possibility Palmer is with a group of Bedouins. Status unknown. Note that all cellphone coverage along route to Khartoum is out. No way to communicate with Acton.

Reading cursed and handed the phone to Leather.

"What is it?" asked Spencer.

"Laura might have been picked up by some Bedouins."

"Isn't that good?"

"It depends if they're friendly or not. There's probably no way to know."

"At least she's alive."

Leather shook his head, returning the phone. "That's not what it says here. It says that she *might* have been picked up by a group of Bedouins. It doesn't say they've confirmed it. My guess is they compared before and after satellite images of the group and found the headcounts didn't match."

193

"But her clothes, wouldn't they be different?"

"They would be, but the fact they're not sure it's her means that whomever they think is her is wearing clothes that have her blending in with the group."

"Why would they do that?"

"Probably so she doesn't stand out."

"That could be a good thing," observed Reading. "They could be hiding her to protect her, though it's just as likely they're hiding her to protect their payday. She speaks Arabic, so if we're lucky, so do they, and she was able to explain her situation to them. I suppose the good news is that if it is her, she's alive." He wagged his phone. "My concern at the moment is Jim. I have to assume that when he reaches the road, he's going to flag someone down in the hopes they'll take him to the GPS coordinates that we have for the crash site. But she's not there anymore, and with the entire cellular network in the area down, we can't let him know."

Leather agreed and Spencer rolled his eyes. "You two are thinking too twentieth century."

Leather cocked an eyebrow and Reading regarded his son. "Oh?"

Spencer smiled. "I assume we have more drones?"

"Several," confirmed Leather.

"Then why don't we combine twenty-first-century technology with twentieth?"

Reading eyed his son. "What are you suggesting?"

"Take a drone, stick a Post-it note on it with what we want him to know, then send it out to Jim's position and drop it right in front of him."

Reading's eyes shot wide as Leather chuckled. "Could it be that simple?"

Leather shrugged. "I don't see why not."

Reading smiled. "Then what are we waiting for?"

En Route to Bedouin Camp

Sudan

Laura walked with the women of the tribe that she wasn't certain were her rescuers or her new captors. She had pled her case, explaining about the hostage situation, about the men planning on raping then killing her, and how her students would be massacred before morning. A discussion had been held between the men in a language she didn't recognize, likely something tribal, then the elder had said something to the women and she was surrounded moments later and fitted with long dark robes. She had asked the woman who had smiled at her earlier, why?

"It's too dangerous for White women to be seen in this area."

"Am I in danger?"

The woman frowned. "Not from us, not yet."

"Not yet?"

"It will be up to the elders what's done with you. Until then, you're under our protection."

The words hadn't provided much comfort. For the moment, it appeared she was protected by Islamic custom. She had been invited to join them, and as with any guest in a Muslim household, they were honor bound to protect her. However, once they reached their destination and the elders conferred, the invitation could be revoked. The question was, what happened then? Was she to be simply killed as an infidel, sent out into the hot desert sun to die, sold to slavers, or turned over to the government?

At the moment, unfortunately, she saw no other option but to stay with them. She checked her watch. The Russian convoy from Khartoum was less than two hours out if the estimates from the CIA were accurate. Once they arrived, they would use her students to finish the work, then when done, execute them. It meant whatever resolution was to be negotiated had to be finished before the day was out. Otherwise, her students' lives were forfeit, and her will to live would be gone.

Bed Chambers of Pharaoh Djoser

Memphis, Old Kingdom

2648 BC

Imhotep's heart ached at the agony on his friend's face as he wretched yet again over the side of his bed, a slave doing her best to catch the mess in a large bowl. Finished, Djoser lay back gasping as the slave rushed away, two more scurrying in to clean the floor, another to wipe their god's face.

"I have the water you requested, sir."

Imhotep turned to see a slave carrying a steaming pot. He pointed at a nearby table. "Place it there."

"What's wrong with me?" gasped Djoser. "I've been sick before, but this is a thousand times worse."

"I'm not sure, sire," replied Imhotep as he stepped over to the table and opened his bag, adding the preparation that would counteract the root inflicting Djoser's stomach. He reached into the bag and gripped the small pouch, the debate still raging.

198

High Priest Neper stepped into the room just to Imhotep's right. Their eyes met briefly and Imhotep averted his gaze. He had to do this. It was his sister's only hope. He grasped the small pouch and untied the drawstring. Using a small spoon, he measured out the dose, double what would be necessary. He could have dumped the entire pouch in, but that would appear suspicious, and now that he was under the watchful eye of the high priest, who himself was skilled in such preparations, he had to be careful.

He stirred the brew then brought it to Djoser. "Drink this, my friend. It will calm your stomach then relax you so you can get some rest. You'll feel your old self by morning."

Djoser pushed up on his elbows and Imhotep pressed the cup to the man's lips, tipping it slightly. His pharaoh took a sip then winced, pulling away. "What are you trying to do, kill me?"

Imhotep's heart nearly stopped.

"That tastes horrible!"

Imhotep forced a smile. "It may taste horrible, but it works quickly. You'll start to feel better before you know it."

Djoser grunted and grabbed the cup, gulping it down, his face scrunched up with displeasure. He finished the brew and handed the cup back to Imhotep. "I much prefer last night's beer." Djoser collapsed onto his bedding, exhausted and covered in sweat. "What do you think's wrong with me?"

"I'm guessing food poisoning."

Neper stepped forward. "Are you suggesting our pharaoh was poisoned?"

Imhotep rapidly shook his head, perhaps a little too rapidly. "No, no, no, not at all. Just a bad bit of food."

"Wouldn't his tasters have become ill as well?"

"It would depend," said Imhotep as he placed the now empty cup in his bag then closed it. "If an entire dish was contaminated, then yes, but it could have been a mere bite. If the tasters sampled a dish from one part of the tray, but it was a different part that was bad, then they would be fine. That being said, it can take time for these things to take effect, and it's different with everyone, so we should monitor those responsible for the food last night."

Djoser reached out for Imhotep. "And you, my friend, how are you feeling?"

"Perfectly fine, though I fear in the morning I'll have a bit of a headache. We did manage to finish off all of the beer I brought."

Djoser chuckled. "It was a fine batch that deserved not to go to waste." He drew a breath and exhaled loudly, placing a hand on his stomach. "Is it possible that I could already be starting to feel better?"

Imhotep smiled. "Possibly, though more likely it's the anticipation of feeling better that you're noticing. I gave you a sedative to help you sleep. I suggest we all leave you alone to rest, and I suspect you'll be fine by sunrise."

Djoser agreed, flicking his wrist at those gathered. "My friend is right. Everyone leave except for you." He indicated Neper. "I think a prayer for my rapid recovery is in order." He smirked at Imhotep. "Despite my complete confidence in my friend's abilities."

Imhotep bowed deeply. "Assistance from the gods is always welcome."

The room emptied and Imhotep made his way out of the palace as quickly as he could without appearing suspicious. He was home in short order, his estate not far from the palace grounds, and entered quietly so as not to wake the household. He headed immediately to his office and rinsed out the cup he had taken, then tossed the pouch with the poison in the fire, the dried leaves flaring briefly.

He sat in his chair and reviewed everything he had done. The beer had been purposely tainted, but it had all been drunk. He had rinsed out the jugs in the brewery, leaving no trace of his treachery, and he had witnessed the servants clearing the empty cups before he left. They would no doubt be washed by now. There should be no possibility of anyone figuring out how Djoser had become ill.

Imhotep had taken the antidote in time, and all present while he treated Djoser were witnesses to the fact the only other person who had the beer wasn't sick. It gave more credibility to his food poisoning theory.

He had destroyed all evidence of the poison he had just administered. Djoser should soon be asleep, but also beginning to feel better, something those attending to him, who would remain despite Djoser's orders for the room to be emptied, would be witness to, which should suggest the preparation he had given their pharaoh wasn't the cause of death.

It was the perfect murder, yet for some reason he had this ominous sense he would be found out. There was something he was forgetting, but he couldn't for the life of him figure out what it was. There was a tap at his door and he flinched, his head spinning toward the sound.

His wife stood in the door frame. "I didn't think I would see you again."

Imhotep rose and took her in his arms. "I wasn't certain you would. I had expected he would want me to stay with him through the night, but instead he agreed to my suggestion that he be left alone and get his rest."

"Thank the gods for that. Is it done?"

He sighed. "My part in it is."

She took his face in her hands and stared up into his eyes. "Then join me in my bed, and let us enjoy one last night together, for I dread what the morning brings."

Road to Khartoum

Sudan

Present Day

Acton reached the road without incident. A couple of miles to his left was the border, and far to his south was the capital of Khartoum. He checked his phone again, confirming there was still no cell coverage. In a perfect world, he would have brought a satellite phone, but the dig only had two. Laura had taken one with her, and the other had to remain with Reading and Leather. The worst-case scenario they had planned on was him being discovered planting the relay. No consideration had been given to the possibility he might go off on his own rescue operation and might need to communicate.

He stared up and down the road. There wasn't a car in sight, and he didn't know why he was surprised. Sudan wasn't exactly a tourist destination, and with the two factions still battling it out, trade was barely a trickle of what it once was. He had two choices. He could head for the border, cross back into Egypt and get picked up by the others, or he could head deeper into the troubled country and pray someone came along that could get him to where he needed to be.

There was really only one choice.

He turned south and headed toward where his wife might be dying.

A whirring sound had him spinning around, and he spotted a drone approaching. His eyes narrowed. "What the hell?"

It came to a halt in front of him and slowly lowered to the ground. He took a knee in front of it, recognizing it as one of the radio-controlled types they used at the dig site. It had to have been sent by Reading and the others. But for what purpose? He picked it up and examined it, spotting nothing unusual, then flipped it over and smiled. There was an envelope taped to the bottom with his name written on it. He gently removed it then opened the envelope and pulled out the contents, a piece of paper. It was a note from his friend. He read it and cursed. Laura likely wasn't at the crash site anymore, and they didn't have new coordinates for her, nor did they know the intent of the Bedouins she might be with.

The good news was that if she were indeed with the Bedouins, then he wasn't in a race to reach her before she succumbed to injuries, but he was still in a race to possibly rescue her, unarmed. Unfortunately, the distances involved were still too great. He held up the drone and stared into the camera.

"If you can hear me, pulse the power."

The blades whirred for a moment.

"Good. I've received your message and for the moment it doesn't change anything, just my ultimate destination. I'm going to keep on this road. Somebody is bound to come along so I can cover the distance quicker. Once I do, however, I'll be out of range of this drone." He stared into the camera. "If you get any new coordinates for her, send the drone to look for me. I might still be close. Doesn't look like there's a lot of traffic here. Wish me luck."

He put the drone down and it lifted off, hovering in front of him for a moment, and he could imagine Reading giving him a stern lecture about not being bloody daft. The drone sped away, returning to Reading and the others, and Acton began the potentially futile hike south.

Operations Center 2, CIA Headquarters

Langley, Virginia

"Status?" asked Director Morrison as he entered the operations center.

Leroux stood and clasped his hands behind his back. "Sir, we just got a shot of Laura Palmer looking up, so we've now confirmed that she is indeed with the group of Bedouins. We've also got a better angle on the crash site and have confirmed two dead Sudanese soldiers inside. It looks like, well, I'm not sure what it looks like."

"Certainly wasn't a car accident that killed them," Child interjected. "It looks like Laura beat them to death."

Morrison grunted. "Nothing would surprise me with that woman. So, she kills her captors. In the process, the vehicle flips on its side, the Bedouins come along and she joins them. Do we know who these people are?"

"Hard to say. They appear to be a Bedouin tribe living the traditional lifestyle. At least some of them likely speak Arabic, and we know Palmer does, so she would be able to communicate with them. She doesn't appear to be bound or restricted in any way, but there's no way to know their ultimate intentions. It's easier to bring a prisoner with you willingly then betray them later."

"Do we know where they're heading?"

"We think so. Randy?"

Child changed the feed, revealing a camp with two dozen large tents. "We believe this is where they're heading," explained Leroux. "They're only a couple of klicks away from it now. They're either rejoining the main body of their tribe, or it's a waypoint. Maybe they're going to do some trading. Either way, I'm guessing this is where they'll be spending the night."

Morrison frowned. "And probably every one of them has a gun. It'd be easier to effect a rescue before they got there."

"Do we have permission for a rescue?"

"We do. A Delta unit is being called up, but they're a couple of hours out, and their job is to rescue the American students plus any other citizens of foreign allies that are with them."

"So, not Palmer."

"Now that she's not with the main body, no. The Brits will have to extract her themselves."

"Do they have a team in position?"

"They're repositioning a unit but they won't be ready for at least eight hours."

Leroux sighed. "We can't just leave Palmer with these people. We have no idea what their intentions are."

"What about Acton?" asked Child.

207

Morrison cocked an eyebrow. "What about him?"

"Well, he's on foot right now, sir, heading south toward his wife's last known position, which to him is the crash site."

Morrison rolled his eyes. "Great. That's the last thing we need. Is there any way he can reach her?"

"If we feed him the new coordinates and the destination is that camp, in theory, he could reach it by tonight."

Morrison frowned. "If he gets himself captured by the Bedouins, then that would put an American citizen with Professor Palmer and we'd be able to send in a team to extract them both. But we couldn't act until he gets there. And that Russian column?"

"Well under two hours."

Morrison cursed. "None of this matters. They'll get there before we can get Delta in, regardless, which means they're taking on twelve former Spetsnaz instead of four. And unless we somehow let Acton know where his wife actually is, we can't pick the two of them up. And I don't even know at the moment if Washington would approve a mission to extract him, seeing as how he went in on his own to rescue his wife."

"Who was a hostage," said Packman. "Would any of us do anything different?"

Morrison regarded the man. "No, I suppose not, but I don't know if Washington's as sentimental as we are." He pointed at the image showing Acton. "See if you can figure out some way to get the new coordinates to him. Otherwise, it doesn't matter."

Road to Khartoum

Sudan

Acton was in a Catch-22. If he walked down the road, he would make better time, but it was hotter, and he would go through his water faster. If he stayed off to the side, it was several degrees cooler, which meant he would need less of his precious water, but it would take him far longer. He made the decision to stick to the road, and as he took another swig, he realized it didn't matter—if he had to walk the whole way, he would be out of water long before he reached his destination no matter what path he chose.

Unfortunately, the sun was still high in the sky and he wouldn't get any relief from it for at least six hours. His only hope was for someone to come along, but the road had remained depressingly empty. At least if somebody had gone by and just ignored him, there would be hope someone else would come and take pity on him. But for all he knew, there were roadblocks set up, turning people around.

He heard a whirring sound behind him and he turned to see the drone approaching once again. He smiled, noticing it was a different model this time. It landed in front of him and he retrieved the message from Reading.

This drone is satellite controlled. With the greater range, we should be able to keep up with you a little bit longer. Good news, CIA has confirmed Laura is alive and is with the Bedouins. They appear to be heading to a Bedouin camp near her current position. Coordinates for the camp below.

Acton glanced to see the coordinates carefully printed at the bottom of the page. He continued reading.

Russian convoy, ETA on your position approximately one hour. Be careful they don't spot you. Possible rescue attempt by Delta on the students within two hours. CIA indicates Delta not authorized to rescue Laura, though suggests that might change if you're with her. British SAS might be able to attempt a rescue overnight. Intent of Bedouins is still not known.

Acton tossed his head back, squeezing his eyes shut. The message was sobering. Laura could still be rescued by a team sent in by her government, but they would be heading into an encampment that could have hundreds of armed men. It could be a blood bath if the Bedouins had hostile intent. He had to get there first. How the hell he was going to manage that, he had no idea.

He heard a noise behind him and spun.

Egypt/Sudan Border

"Get out of sight."

Reading turned to Leather. "What did he say?"

Leather manipulated the controls of the drone. "He said, 'Get out of sight.'"

Reading watched the camera feed, the drone lifting off and speeding away before turning back to see Acton waving not at them, but at someone else. "Who's he waving at?"

Leather panned the camera to the left then Spencer pointed. "There!"

Leather zoomed in, the camera revealing two camels, one carrying what appeared to be a Bedouin, the other laden with goods.

Spencer leaned in. "What do you think the chances are this dude's heading right for that camp Laura's being held at?"

Reading grunted. "I think the chances are pretty damn good. But even if he isn't, if Jim can hitch a ride, it at least gives him a chance of making it there in time." He watched as a conversation took place between Acton and the new arrival, and smiled as minutes later his friend was outfitted

211

in flowing black robes then helped atop the second camel. Fist bumps were exchanged between him, Spencer, and Leather.

"I guess we'd better let the CIA know," said Spencer.

Reading laughed. "Trust me, they already know." He turned to Leather. "Now what?"

"With your permission, I want to prepare my team to assist in the rescue operation should it become necessary."

Reading pursed his lips. "What did you have in mind?"

"I have four highly skilled former operators with me, equipped with weapons capable of making a difference if we get in close enough."

"So, across the border."

"Yes."

Reading considered the idea for a moment. Sending five men in against four Spetsnaz, a helicopter, and at least half a dozen Sudanese wouldn't be wise. Add a Delta team, and the odds evened out dramatically. He finally gave a curt nod. "Prep your men."

Bedouin Camp

Sudan

Shouts erupted and scores of women and children emerged from the tents, rushing to greet the new arrivals. Laura's heart pounded with trepidation. Now that she was here, a decision on her fate would be made. As men appeared, all carrying Kalashnikov variants, her apprehension grew. But along with it came an idea. She counted at least fifty men, all armed, far outnumbering the Russians and Sudanese back at the dig. Could she persuade these people to help her?

She dismissed the idea. Numbers were one thing, but as the Russians had proved in Ukraine, numbers could just mean more cannon fodder if they weren't properly trained and equipped. She couldn't get them involved. The Spetsnaz team could decimate them.

And then there was the helicopter she had forgotten about.

No. The most she could ask of these people was that they bring her to the border so she could contact James and get picked up. The elder she had spoken to, whom she had been informed by one of the women was named Salah, was embraced by a group of men, clearly the elders referred to earlier. He indicated her with a wave of his hand, triggering a conversation in their native language. A word was said and one of the men spat, followed by the rest. It had them angry, and her chest tightened, praying things weren't about to take a turn for the worse.

USS Dwight D. Eisenhower
Red Sea

Command Sergeant Major Burt "Big Dog" Dawson leaned against the railing of the USS Dwight D. Eisenhower, staring out at the waters of the Red Sea, enjoying a moment of relaxation. It had been a hectic week, the collapse of control in Sudan rapid and unexpected. A large extraction operation had been mounted, pulling out thousands of Americans and foreign nationals, with dozens of follow-up missions constantly on the go. This was different than the Charlie Foxtrot that was Afghanistan. There were no artificial deadlines and the warring parties on the ground didn't consider America their enemy. As leader of Bravo Team, an elite group of Special Forces operators commonly known to the public as the Delta Force, more formally known as 1st Special Forces Operational Detachment-Delta, he had participated in several ops, and so far no one had fired a shot. Normally that would be considered a boring mission, but in this case, when you were rescuing civilians, it was exactly what you hoped for.

His best friend and second-in-command, Master Sergeant Mike "Red" Belme, joined him. "Penny for your thoughts?"

Dawson grunted. "With inflation, that's not getting you much these days."

Red chuckled. "Too true. If I didn't know this was a short-term phenomenon, I'd be retiring and buying chickens so I could sell the damn eggs and retire a wealthy man."

"Small flaw in that plan."

"What's that?"

"You have to feed the chickens something, and that's way more expensive than it was just a year ago."

Red sighed. "There's always a flaw in the plan."

Sergeants Carl "Niner" Sung and Leon "Atlas" James approached. "Is this a private party?" asked Niner, the team's wise ass.

Dawson flicked a wrist. "Nope, we were just discussing the price of eggs."

Atlas replied with a voice so deep, Dawson was sure it contributed to the vibrations of the deck plating. "Don't get me started on eggs. That's one of my go-to sources of protein. Now they're so damn expensive, when Vanessa makes me an omelet, she sets the table with our finest dinnerware and candles because at those prices, it might as well be fine dining."

The diminutive Niner grinned at his impossibly muscled best friend. "So, what you're saying is that the way into your pants now is through a carton of eggs?"

Atlas gave him a look. "Don't you get started or I'll toss you overboard."

Niner clasped his hands in front of his heart, tilting his head to the side and batting his eyes. "Oh, if my last memory was of being manhandled by you, I'd die a happy man."

Red snorted and Atlas growled menacingly.

Sergeant Will "Spock" Lightman jogged over. "Hey, BD, we've got another op."

Everyone faced Spock, the teasing put on hold. "What do we know?" asked Dawson.

"You're not going to believe this one. They're not sending us in to pick up people who missed the initial extraction. We're going in to pick up people who voluntarily entered the country this morning and have been taken hostage."

Niner rolled his eyes. "What kind of morons voluntarily go into a FUBAR country like Sudan is right now?"

"Would you believe Professors Laura Palmer and James Acton, along with five of their students?"

Dawson groaned at the mention of the professors they all now considered friends, despite the fact the team had spent the better part of a week trying to kill them during their first encounter. It was false intel that had them acting on orders that Acton was the leader of a domestic terror cell. Too many innocents had died, and his team still wasn't square with the professors. If they needed help, there wasn't a member of Bravo Team who wouldn't drop everything for them.

"Which side is holding them?"

"Oh, you're going to love this. Remember that group of art thieves, former Spetsnaz that we last had a run-in with in Ethiopia?"

Niner spat. "Russians. Patton was right. We should have taken them on after we finished with the Nazis." He turned to Dawson. "Please tell me we can kill them all this time."

Dawson started heading inside. "We'll have to see what our ROEs say, but if Washington gives the okay, I'm all for it."

Bedouin Camp

Sudan

Fortunately, all the elders spoke Arabic, and after Laura explained the situation in detail and answered their questions, it was clear what had the men so agitated. It was the mention of the Russians. Every time the word was uttered, there was a collective spit from all the men gathered. It had become almost comical, though she didn't dare smile and trivialize their hatred. The fact their anger was directed at her enemy was a relief, and it suggested she might get the help she needed.

"Will you take me to the border?"

The elder she had met at the crash site, Salah, nodded. "Yes, but first you must tell us where these Russians are. They're responsible for killing many of our brothers and sisters in Libya. They must be dealt with first."

Her stomach churned. If these men attacked the Russians at the dig, her students could very likely be killed, for this wouldn't be a disciplined rescue operation. It would merely be thousands of rounds sprayed indiscriminately, hoping to hit something. "I think it's best that we leave this to my government. A lot of you could get killed."

Salah peered into her eyes. "To die in service to Allah is every man's dream. Do not concern yourself with such things as our lives."

"I'm more concerned with the lives of my students. They could get killed in the crossfire."

"But they too will have died in an honorable battle, and even though they are infidels, Allah will make accommodations for them."

She needed a way out, a way that wouldn't offend these people. Then a thought occurred to her. "You want to kill Russians?"

The men nodded and she pointed back toward the road. "There's a convoy on the way from Khartoum. It'll be here within an hour. It has eight Russians on their way to join the four Russians that are holding my people. They have an escort of Sudanese soldiers. I don't know how many. It'll be dangerous, and I still think you shouldn't do it, but if you really want to kill Russians, then I would suggest attacking the convoy that has twice as many and no innocent students."

The discussion switched back to their native tongue and she stood waiting for a decision, her stomach roiling as she battled the bile filling her mouth. Whoever died in the upcoming battle, their blood was on her hands.

Hands were shook and orders were shouted as Salah turned, a rotting smile directed at her. "It is decided. We shall attack this convoy." He thrust his AK-47 in the air and shouted, "Allahu Akbar!" and Laura forced a smile as the torment gripping her threatened to make her physically ill.

Operations Center 2, CIA Headquarters
Langley, Virginia

Leroux stared at the screen. Tong and the rest sent to get some shut-eye were back, but there was no time for the rest of them. Delta was already inbound and had been seconded to the CIA for the duration of the op. He had worked with Bravo Team countless times and was ecstatic they were the ones assigned to the mission. Not only was he confident they would succeed like any other American Special Forces team would, but because they were so close with the professors, there was no way they were leaving them hanging because of politics.

"Looks like they're up to something," said Tong, gesturing at the screen.

Leroux looked up from an email Morrison had sent confirming Washington had already indicated Acton was on his own unless he encountered hostiles. He had a feeling Bravo Team would figure out a way around that if it became necessary.

"So, where do you think they're headed?" asked Child. "Has Palmer whipped them up into a frenzy to go rescue her students?"

Leroux couldn't see it. It was too dangerous, and she would have to know that rescue plans would already be underway. "Let's hope not. It could just get those students killed."

Tong faced him. "She's a smart cookie. She would know that."

"Agreed."

"So, if they're not going to rescue the students, what do you think they're doing?"

Leroux scratched his five o'clock shadow. "Show me where she is and where that convoy is."

Tong updated the main display.

He rose and pointed. "Fifty bucks says they're going to hit that convoy."

"To what end?"

"I don't know. I can't see it being her idea. As soon as that convoy is hit, they're going to radio their situation to their buddies, and that could put the students' lives at risk."

"Maybe they hate Russians just as much as we do," suggested Child, jokingly, as he spun in his chair.

Leroux snapped his fingers. "That's it. Russians, especially Wagner Group, have killed thousands in Libya, including a lot of Bedouins. Laura would've mentioned the Russians and they'd be horny to kill them if they got a chance. Laura would know an attack at the students' location would be too dangerous, so she would've probably encouraged them to hit the convoy instead. All right, let's assume they're hitting the convoy. Let's get some more precise time estimates here. I want to know exactly when we think the convoy's going to reach the most likely interception point, and when Delta's going to reach the primary site. I need to know how big a gap we've got, because the longer it is, the worse it could get for the hostages."

Morrison entered the room and Leroux rose. The Chief stared at the display, his eyebrows narrowing at the shot of the Bedouins mounting up for battle. "What the hell's going on?"

"We think the Bedouins are going to attack the convoy."

"Why would they do that?"

"The going theory is that they found out there are Russians in it."

Morrison groaned. "Lovely. This day just keeps getting better and better."

Leroux detected the frustration in the man's voice. "What's the word?"

"The official Sudanese government response is that Palmer and her students were in their territory illegally despite the fact they had visas. The Sudanese say those visas were illegitimate and were revoked before they crossed the border. The Russians are there legitimately at the request of the Sudanese government for their archaeological expertise, and any interference will be considered an aggressive act. The students aren't in any danger and will be released as soon as possible."

Leroux frowned. "Do you believe them?"

"Not for a second. I don't think they had a clue anybody was there until we told them. But it looks like the Russians laid one hell of a bribe on some very senior Sudanese officials, far higher than Palmer's contacts managed."

"Does that mean Delta's standing down?"

"Not yet. The Egyptians have granted permission for Delta to hold on their side of the border should it become necessary to go in." Morrison jabbed a finger at the display. "But if those yahoos attack that convoy, it could change the entire nature of this situation."

En Route to Bedouin Camp
Sudan

Acton was tired, sore, hot, and sweaty. But he was alive, heading in the right direction a hell of a lot faster than on foot, with food and water that would far outlast the limited supply he had brought. The Bedouin he had encountered was a man of few words, and once they had been underway, nothing had been said between the two of them. Unfortunately, this left him alone with his thoughts, and he couldn't help but worry about Laura and the students.

He glanced up and to his right, and spotted the drone following them. It provided him with some comfort knowing his friend was watching, but unfortunately, it couldn't provide any help.

The Bedouin had indicated he knew where the camp was that the CIA had indicated Laura was at, and that he would take him there. Unfortunately, there was no sense of urgency in their pace, though it was dramatically faster than walking in the hot sun.

He checked his phone, having punched in the new GPS coordinates provided by Reading in the last message. They had already covered half the distance. He could urge his camel forward, the awkwardly swift creature potentially getting him there in fifteen minutes. But that would have him charging alone into a camp of people likely well-armed and distrusting of strangers, especially Westerners. No, the best thing for him to do right now was to remain with this man, and enter the camp with what was hopefully a familiar face who could make introductions.

He just prayed that when he did arrive, Laura was unharmed and there as a guest, not a prisoner. But at least with Reading's watchful eye from the satellite-controlled drone, if he were taken prisoner, it should merit a rescue attempt for both of them.

Gunfire erupted ahead and Acton's heart leaped into his throat. He was well aware they were in a race against time, with the second group of Russians due to arrive shortly. He recognized the distinctive rattle of Kalashnikovs, probably AK-47s. He was aware Spetsnaz preferred AK-74 variants, but these particular Russians likely used something more exotic, so what he was hearing was probably Bedouins, rebels, or the Sudanese army. This was likely a battle between locals best avoided, and it appeared his partner agreed, bringing his camel to a halt.

He turned toward Acton. "We should get off the road."

Acton agreed, and was about to follow the man when different weapons joined the fight, the sound something he recognized from his last encounter with the Russians in Ethiopia.

HKs.

It was the Russian convoy, and that meant Laura might somehow be involved.

Ambush Site

Sudan

Laura rushed forward and grabbed the AK-47 lying on the ground, its previous owner dead. She dove behind a rock, checking the weapon as the disaster continued to unfold around her. The Bedouins, clearly inexperienced in battle, were consumed with hate, all their firepower aimed at the Russians in their distinctive gear. By ignoring the Sudanese troops, it allowed the Russians' escorts to open fire at will, mowing down the bulk of the initial wave.

She popped up and took aim at one of the trailing escorts, a .50 cal mounted in the back spewing death. She squeezed the trigger, taking out the gunner, then dropped back down. The Russians had remained buttoned up in their vehicles for the first thirty to sixty seconds while those leading the ambush were thinned out, then they had joined in with deadly consequences, the well-trained men eliminating at least two dozen of the Bedouins as they rolled past, the convoy barely slowing.

The remanned .50 opened up again and she rose, taking out the new gunner, the weapon silenced once and for all, at least in this battle. As the trailing vehicle raced out of range, she rose along with the few survivors, shaking her head in disbelief at the waste, at the carnage that surrounded her. Dozens were dead or dying uselessly, and as far as she could tell, not a single Russian had even been wounded, and the only two dead on the Sudanese side might have been her two kills.

It was an unmitigated disaster, though because of it, because the ambush had been so inexpertly executed and the consequences almost entirely one-sided, it would hopefully be clear to the Russians that this had nothing to do with a coordinated rescue attempt for her students. Hopefully, it would mean that this foolish action wouldn't cost her students their lives.

Gunfire erupted down the road and Laura peered into the distance, wondering what poor soul the enemy was firing at now.

Acton dove off his camel, hitting the ground hard. He rolled to his feet and sprinted away from the road, keeping the camel between him and the convoy as best he could. He spotted a boulder and leaped over it as gunfire tore apart the ground around him. He curled up into a ball, making as small a target as possible as the barrage continued, the sound changing with the Doppler effect as the convoy raced past.

He shifted his position slightly, keeping the stone between him and the wall of lead before the weapons fell silent and the convoy rolled out of sight. He listened for any more engines but heard nothing. He pushed to a knee, surveying the area, and his shoulders slumped at the sight of his camel, dead on the side of the road. The moment he had heard the Russian weapons, he had abandoned the Bedouin and set off at a full gallop instead of taking cover as instructed. The camel was dead because of him, and the poor Bedouin deserved compensation.

But that would have to wait, for he needed to find out who had been involved in the battle just down the road. He set off at a jog, determined to discover if the woman he loved had somehow been caught up in whatever had happened.

Egypt/Sudan Border

"What the hell does he think he's doing?" exclaimed Reading, tossing his hands in the air as they watched Acton running down the road, having just narrowly escaped death.

Leather shook his head. "It doesn't make sense. You would think he'd go back and check on the guy he was with."

Spencer shrugged. "Maybe he just assumes he'll catch up."

"Maybe, but why is he running?"

Reading snapped his fingers. "Something else must have happened. There's no reason for the Russians to have shot at him. He's dressed as a local. Something must have spooked them."

Leather cursed. "If the Bedouins attacked the convoy, it would be close enough for Jim to hear it, and it would obviously put the Russians on alert against any other Bedouins."

"Send the drone ahead," urged Reading, his foot bouncing with impatience.

Leather complied and the drone was soon racing ahead, gaining altitude, and a collective gasp escaped all those watching as dozens of bodies, some writhing on the ground, others still, came into view. Weapons were strewn about, dozens swarming the area attending to the wounded, the microphone picking up the anguished wails of the newly widowed as they found the bodies of their husbands and draped themselves over their corpses.

Nobody said anything, no one trusting their voices wouldn't crack at the horror. Reading desperately wanted to block the image so his son couldn't see it, but his boy was a man now, and this was the reality of the world everyone lived in. Whether it was the shopping malls and schools of America, or the desert of Africa, this was the bloody reality. There was no protecting him from it.

Leather was the first to break the silence. "It was a blood bath. They didn't stand a chance."

Spencer, his eyes still wide from the shock, murmured. "Why would they do it?"

Reading sighed. "I don't know. They might have thought they were helping, though I can't see Laura intentionally getting them involved. She would know what they were up against."

One of the figures peered up at the drone, shielding their eyes from the sun, and relief swept through Reading as he recognized Laura.

"That's her!" exclaimed Spencer with excitement, pointing at the screen.

"And it looks like she was involved." Reading frowned at the sight of an AK-47 gripped in the woman's hand, but he was still convinced this wasn't her doing. She likely participated only to even out the odds, apparently to no avail. "Can you do some sort of wing wag or something to let her know it's us?"

"I could drop it right down in front of her like we did with Jim."

"No, that whole group is on edge right now. They'll blow the thing out of the sky, and we need it to see what's going on."

"You're right." Leather manipulated the controls and Laura waved.

"All right, let's get back to Jim. Let's see if we can slow him up a bit so he doesn't run headlong into that group and get himself killed."

Exploratory Site

Sudan

Tankov cursed at the update radioed in from the convoy. They had been ambushed by Bedouins barely ten miles from here. It was an attack with numbers, though piss-poorly executed. Two Sudanese were dead, but all of his men were intact as was their equipment. He called over Colonel Abdeen who likely was unaware of what had happened, his men using primitive radios whereas Tankov's team were all on SATCOMs.

"Yes, what is it?"

"I just received an update from the convoy. It appears they were ambushed by Bedouins."

The colonel's eyes narrowed. "Bedouins? That's unusual. They usually keep to themselves. Are they sure it wasn't rebel forces?"

"No. Even if they were in disguise, they would've done a better job than this. I regret to inform you that two of your men were killed, but dozens of the enemy died in exchange."

Abdeen frowned. "Regrettable. The status of the convoy?"

"Still en route. The attack barely delayed them. They'll be here on schedule."

Abdeen turned toward the students digging away in the sand nearby, the top of a car already revealed. It was an encouraging sign that the contents of Imhotep's tomb were indeed buried here in this forgotten gorge. When the equipment got here, they would make quick work of the area. If there was nothing to find, they would be gone in a couple of hours. But if there was indeed something here, they could be here for days.

He had to assume by now that the Americans had eyes on them. He had found the team's satphone, hidden in the Mercedes, with a message from Acton indicating they were aware of what was going on. As soon as they were aware something was wrong, they would have contacted the authorities, and with how well-connected the professors were, he had no doubt Washington was pulling out all the stops. But there was no way the Bedouins were part of any American rescue plan. With what was going on in the region, substantial numbers of American Special Forces were in the area and could be arriving at any moment. But an all-out attack rather than a negotiation wouldn't make sense.

"Tell your men to keep their eyes open. Those Bedouins could be out for revenge."

Abdeen beckoned the captain while Tankov joined his men and filled them in on what had just been reported. "Keep your eyes out for any Bedouins approaching. I don't think this has anything to do with any rescue op, but if we just killed a few dozen of their brothers, they might decide to pay us a visit."

Utkin grunted. "Then they're going to lose a hell of a lot more than that if they do."

"Agreed. Let's just keep our eyes open for anything unusual. We know the Americans are coming eventually, so let's watch the sky too. No surprises."

En Route to Bedouin Camp
Sudan

The drone rapidly approached then stopped directly in front of Acton. He pulled up from his sprint that had turned into a jog, the heat having sapped him of too much of his stamina.

"Okay, what's up?" he asked uselessly, making a mental note that the next model of drone they bought should have two-way communications. "Yes, I'm heading toward the gunfire. I'm going to assume you've seen it."

The engines revved once and he smiled. "Okay, let's go Captain Pike. One rev for 'Yes,' two revs for 'No.' You've seen what's ahead?"

Single rev.

"Is the battle over?"

Single rev.

He sucked in a breath. "Was Laura involved?" His chest ached at the single rev. "Is she all right?" Another single rev had him sighing in relief, clasping his heart. "Oh, thank God! Is it safe to proceed?"

237

The drone wagged from side to side and Acton chuckled. "So-so? Maybe?"

A single rev.

"Okay, I'll take that to mean proceed with caution, so I won't run into the area. Now, get out of my way."

The drone swerved to the side and Acton resumed his jog, excitement overcoming his fear of what lay ahead with the knowledge that Laura would be there and was all right. He spotted something ahead and slowed. People were milling about at the side of the road. Women wailed and men groaned in agony. He raised his hands high in the air and continued forward, the stench of death reaching his nostrils. Whatever had happened here had been a massacre.

Someone noticed him and shouted, half a dozen men rushing into position to protect the others.

"James, is that you?"

He gasped at Laura's voice. "Yes! It's me!"

"That's my husband!" shouted Laura in Arabic, and a figure dressed like a local raced toward him. He cried out and grabbed her as she rushed into his arms. He held her tight, picking her up off the ground before staring into her eyes.

"I was afraid I was never going to see you again."

She stared back, her eyes filled with tears. "For a little while, I was thinking the same thing."

He let go and she swatted his chest. "What are you doing here? Are you daft?"

He grinned. "I think we established that years ago. Can't you tell? I'm here to rescue you."

She laughed. "You and what army?"

Acton jerked a thumb at the drone behind him. "Just the two of us."

"I assume Hugh is at the other end of that?"

"Yes." Acton gestured toward the bloody scene. "What happened here?"

Laura sighed. "They heard there were Russians in the convoy, so they decided to ambush it despite me begging them not to."

"I take it it didn't go well?"

"It was horrible. I managed to take out two of the Sudanese, but that's about it."

"Yeah, they tried to take me out about a mile down the road." He indicated his robes. "They must have thought I was one of them."

"Are my students all right?"

"As far as I know, yes. Delta is on its way, but I don't know exactly what's happening. We've got one-way communication with Hugh, so we'll let him know our status and he can radio it back to the CIA, and they can arrange a pickup and get us back on the Egyptian side of the border."

"Whatever they're going to do, they have to do it quickly."

Acton eyed Laura. "What do you mean?"

"I mean, these people have already sent out runners. They're gathering all the Bedouin tribes in the area and they're going to attack the Russians for revenge for what happened here. If they do, it'll be another blood bath, and my students could get caught in the crossfire."

Acton cursed and beckoned the drone. "We need to let the CIA know what's coming before it's too late."

Operations Center 2, CIA Headquarters
Langley, Virginia

Leroux cursed as he tore his headset off, tossing it onto his station, the update from Reading more bad news. According to Laura Palmer, the Bedouins were planning on assaulting the dig site in revenge for the disastrous ambush on the convoy, and the Sudanese planned to kill all the students. He turned to Tong. "Agent Reading just relayed a message from Professor Palmer. Apparently, the Bedouins are gathering with plans to attack the dig site. I want our satellite footage analyzed for the entire area. Identify any Bedouin camps that would be able to get forces to the site within the next two hours."

"I'm on it."

"ETA on the convoy?"

Child responded behind him. "They just arrived." He gestured at the display. "And it looks like they're in a hurry."

Leroux directed his attention to the drone feed, the large machine they weren't certain as to its purpose already off the flatbed and moving into position where the captive students had been digging.

"Delta?"

"Ninety minutes to their hold position just across the border in Egypt."

"Is there any way to get them in sooner?"

"Not substantially. We could order the pilot to increase speed, but they're already going pretty much near their max. You might shave five minutes off."

"I want those five minutes."

"Making the call."

Leroux walked over to Tong's station and leaned over, staring at her screens. "Anything?"

"You're not going to like it." She pointed at the screen on her left, over a dozen circles shown on the satellite image. "These are what the computer has identified as possible targets. The ones in green I've confirmed as Bedouin encampments. The ones in red aren't, and the grays I'm still looking at."

"And they're all within two hours of the dig?"

"Yes, and I've reviewed footage from earlier. Almost immediately after the ambush, riders were sent out in every direction. Some have already reached a few of the closest encampments, and there's already activity."

"What about where the professors are?"

She tapped her keyboard and brought up the feed. "It looks like they're still licking their wounds, but camels and horses are being readied. The survivors look like they'll be heading out soon."

Leroux sighed. "This is not going to end well."

Marc Therrien groaned from the back of the room. "Hey, boss, you're not going to like this."

"What?"

"The Sudanese have just dispatched a column from their base at Shaddah, along with two attack helicopters."

Leroux closed his eyes for a moment. "Destination?"

"Can't say for sure, but they're definitely headed in the right direction to cause trouble."

"ETA?"

"One hour. Those choppers can be there in ten minutes. For the moment, it looks like they're flying escort."

Leroux returned to his station and dropped into his chair. "So, we've got the full Russian contingent there, plus both Sudanese escorts, a Sudanese column of how many?"

"Looks like at least fifty personnel."

"So, another fifty-plus coming in, one chopper on scene, two more on the way, plus God knows how many Bedouins hell-bent on revenge who won't care who they're shooting, and a Delta team arriving after most of the potential combatants are in the area."

"Those students don't stand a chance," muttered Child, and Leroux had to agree.

243

He closed his eyes and rested his chin on his clasped hands, desperately searching for a solution.

Tong turned towards him. "The Sudanese better do everything they can to protect those students if they know what's good for them."

Leroux opened his eyes and faced her, folding his arms. "Unfortunately, according to Professor Palmer, the Sudanese intend to kill the students."

"But there's no value in killing them."

"Not from the Russian perspective, no. It'll just make every law enforcement agency in the world hunt them down with even more urgency. My guess is Interpol would issue Red Notices on all of them."

"Exactly, so they have to know it's in their best interest to make sure the students remain alive. Maybe they don't know what the Sudanese have planned."

Leroux's head bobbed in agreement. Tong was right. Perhaps it was time to open the lines of communication directly rather than hope Washington might negotiate something with Khartoum.

Child whistled then jerked his chin toward the display. "Well, we were wondering what that thing did."

Leroux's eyes shot wide as the large piece of equipment brought in on the Antonov did its job. "Holy shit, I didn't even know something like that existed."

Exploratory Site

Sudan

Tankov watched as his men operated what Utkin affectionately called the Suck-and-Blow machine. Two of his men controlled one end of a large hose sucking up the sand in front of the nozzle. Two more men on a second hose sprayed the moved sand to a separate area. It eliminated the need to dig, and they could rapidly clear a massive amount of sand out of the way. The students had done a good job revealing the car, but it contained little of interest besides the body of the driver. There were no valuables inside.

They were now focusing on what lay in front of the car. Interrogation of the students indicated there should be a buried Nazi convoy trapped in what was once a gorge. If the students were right, the trapped convoy contained his payday, perhaps the biggest of his career, but time was of the essence here. Operational security was slipping. Bedouins had attacked the convoy for no apparent reason, and he had no doubt word was going out to surrounding tribes to organize some sort of revenge mission. It had prompted Colonel Abdeen to call in reinforcements, and that meant more would know about their little operation. That would mean bigger payouts, but it also raised the risk of the Sudanese turning on them, especially if they found something of significant value.

This was supposed to be nice and clean. Get in, grab whatever there was to grab, then get out. The students weren't a concern. His intent had been just to leave them behind. But the last time the subject had come up, Abdeen had merely said, "They're prisoners of the Sudanese government and none of your concern," which wasn't good.

His cellphone beeped with a message and his eyebrows shot up as all of his men received one at the same time. He pulled out his phone and smirked.

Mr. Tankov, we need to speak.

Utkin walked over. "Who do you think it is?"

"I'm guessing it's the Americans."

"How are they able to send us all a message here in the middle of nowhere?"

Tankov jerked his thumb at the convoy. "When the rest of the team arrived, so did our comms setup. We've got a hotspot now, so all of our phones are connected to the Internet and to the cellular network through a sat relay. They probably just scanned the area to see what devices were pinging, then sent a text message to all of them." He noticed the Suck-and-Blow machine had stopped working. "Everybody back to work!"

The machine cranked up again and phones were returned to pockets.

"What are you going to do?" asked Utkin.

"I'm going to see what they want. As long as we're talking, we're not shooting." Tankov headed away from the noise. He tapped the phone number in the message and the call was immediately answered.

"Mr. Tankov, I presume?"

Tankov smiled and looked up at the sky, giving a wave at whoever was watching him. "You have me at a disadvantage. What should I call you?"

"You can call me Barry."

Tankov laughed. "All right, *Barry*, what can I do for you?"

"Release the hostages immediately."

"And why would I do that?"

"Because if anything happens to them, Interpol will be issuing Red Notices on all of your team members, and you'll be hunted down until every last one of you is caught and put in prison for the rest of your lives."

"What makes you think anything's going to happen to the hostages? As long as your people don't do anything stupid, I intend to release them when I'm done. Right now, they're my guests. Actually, they're the guests of the Sudanese government. I have nothing to do with them being held."

"We both know you're in control of what's happening there. If you tell the Sudanese to let them go, they'll let them go."

"All the more incentive for you to leave us alone. Let us do our job. When we're done, our need for them is done."

"So, they're human shields."

"A barbaric term, though accurate. Just keep your people out of the area and everything will be just fine."

"It's obvious your situational awareness is lacking."

Tankov cocked an eyebrow. "Oh?"

"I assume your men told you about the ambush."

"They told me of an unsuccessful attempt to hijack our convoy. My understanding is it didn't end well for the other side."

"No, it didn't. In fact, it ended so poorly, messengers have been sent out to all the surrounding tribes and they're already mobilizing. They'll be converging on your position within the next hour or two, hundreds of armed men seeking revenge."

Tankov tensed but didn't betray his true feelings at this new bit of intel. "They must like to die."

"And there's another thing you should know."

"What's that?"

"They weren't trying to hijack your little convoy. They found out there were Russians in it. These Bedouins in the area are related to those in Libya that Russian mercenaries slaughtered. Those that'll be attacking you have no interest in negotiating, no interest in what you have. All they want are Russian heads. Now, as soon as the Sudanese realize this, how long do you think it'll be before they turn on you?"

Tankov frowned and stared at Colonel Abdeen. "Don't you worry about us. We can handle them."

"You are aware that over fifty additional troops are on their way, along with two gunships?"

Tankov frowned. Barry was extremely well-informed. He had to be CIA.

"And there's another thing you should know. Professor Palmer escaped."

Tankov's eyebrows shot up.

I love that woman.

"May I ask how?"

"She killed her captors after she found out they planned to rape then kill her, just like your Sudanese friends plan to do with the students."

Tankov bristled. "What?"

"Your Sudanese partners intend to kill all the students. They were never leaving there alive."

Tankov chewed his cheek for a moment. "Unfortunately, if that's what the Sudanese want to do with their prisoners, there's nothing I can do about it."

"That may be. However, know this, those students wouldn't be in the situation they're in if it weren't for you. Therefore, you will be held responsible for anything that does happen to them. If I were you, sir, I'd be trying to figure out a way to get myself and those students out of there before it's too late."

Tankov pursed his lips. "I'll call you back." He ended the call then faced the bustle of activity. Five of his men were working the dig and six were on watch. Most of the Sudanese weren't paying any attention to the perimeter anymore. His men could easily take them out, pack up, and leave. All the students would have to do was head back across the border, where he had no doubt people from their original dig were waiting.

But that would mean abandoning their payday. The only way they could get it out of the country was with the cooperation of the Sudanese. A thought occurred to him. What if it was a bluff? What if everything he had just been told was a lie designed to get him to leave and free the students? If Laura Palmer had indeed escaped, and what she claimed was true, it changed everything. She had been sent away with two guards only minutes into the operation. It meant the Sudanese, right from the get-go, had intended to betray them, which didn't make much sense, for Abdeen and his men had no idea the students were going to be there.

And it had him wondering, had she overheard her captors saying they were going to kill all the students, or that they were going to kill all the foreigners? He stared at Abdeen. Had that bastard planned on betraying them right from the beginning, deciding to take anything they found buried in the sand and kill them all, keeping it for himself? And if he had, what could be done about it? They could kill all the Sudanese now and leave, or let things play out, risking the students' lives and their own. And if they did survive, but the students didn't, they faced arrest and imprisonment.

He frowned, uncertain as to what to do, for whatever he decided could affect the rest of their lives.

Bedouin Camp

Sudan

Eyes bulged as Acton handed over a fistful of American dollars to the poor Bedouin whose camel had been shot due to the unwise charge toward the gunfire. It was enough to buy the man ten or twenty camels in the market, and his anger when he had first arrived at the encampment was erased. Acton shook the man's hand then rejoined Laura.

"Any luck?"

"No. They insist on attacking the dig site." She gestured at several new arrivals. "Apparently, three other camps have already agreed to send men. They can't wait to get a chance to kill the Russians."

"And what do they have to say about the students?"

"Basically, that if it's God's will, they'll survive."

Acton sighed heavily. He never understood religious zealotry, whether it was Middle Eastern or American. Faith was one thing, but blind faith was something entirely different. "What do you want to do?"

251

She shrugged. "There's nothing we can do here. There's no talking them out of what they're about to do."

Acton spotted the now semi-wealthy Bedouin negotiating the purchase of a replacement beast of burden. "Then I think we should head back to the Egyptian side of the border and rejoin Hugh and the others."

"I think you're right."

"Good. I'm going to see a man about a horse."

En Route to Sudan

Command Sergeant Major Dawson frowned as he read the latest update from Control, who in this case was Chris Leroux, a man he had dealt with on many occasions, and had every confidence in his capabilities. And Leroux's assessment of the situation was bleak.

"What's up?" asked Niner, the rest of the team in the cabin of the Black Hawk falling silent.

Dawson held up his secure tablet. "Langley's just informed me that not only are we going up against a dozen Spetsnaz plus a dozen Sudanese with one chopper already on site, but the Bedouins attempted to ambush the Russian convoy and paid a very heavy price for it, so now they've called in tribes from all around the area for some sort of revenge mission."

Red frowned. "ETA?"

"Hard to say. Apparently, some are already moving into position. Whatever's going down, could be going down within an hour, two tops. But that's not all."

Atlas groaned. "It never is."

"That's why we get paid the big bucks," said Sergeant Gerry "Jimmy Olsen" Hudson.

Spock cocked an eyebrow. "You get paid big bucks? We're comparing pay stubs next week."

Dawson continued. "We've got a Sudanese column that's less than an hour out. Two escort gunships plus at least fifty regulars. We don't know exactly whose side they're on, but it might not matter, because they definitely won't be on the Bedouin side."

Niner held up a hand. "Wait a minute. So, we've got God knows how many Bedouins converging on the position. Fifty-plus Sudanese joining a dozen Sudanese and a dozen former Spetsnaz. And the twelve of us have to try to rescue five students in the middle of that mess." He tapped his watch. "And I say in the middle, because I don't think we're getting there before them."

"We're not."

"So, what's the plan?"

"Control has reached out to Tankov, told him what's coming, and told him his men will be held personally responsible if anything happens to the students. Unfortunately, we have a new bit of intel from Laura that indicates the Sudanese intend to kill the students, and always had."

Red shook his head. "I assume Control is hoping to stir dissension within the ranks, but if I were Tankov, I'd be taking anything I was told with a grain of salt."

"So would I," agreed Dawson. "And don't forget, there's the greed element. If they find something at that site, they're not going to want to leave. My concern isn't the Russians, the Sudanese, or the Bedouins. They can kill each other for all I care. That's not our fight. It's the thousands of stray bullets that are going to be flying all over that place. We've got five innocents that will likely get mowed down."

"Then what do you want to do?"

Dawson stared at his tablet, a map of the area displayed. "I think we need to change tactics. We were supposed to be a last resort if negotiations failed. Now we have to assume they've already failed."

"What are you saying?" asked Red.

"I'm saying we're not going to Egypt." He tapped the tablet. "We're heading straight into the belly of the beast."

Egypt/Sudan Border

"Where do you think they're heading?" asked Spencer as they watched Acton and Laura leave the Bedouin camp on horseback.

"Looks like they're heading for the road," said Leather. "Let's hope they're going to take it straight to the border."

Reading grunted. "I wouldn't count on it. Those two are liable to head for the dig site and attempt to rescue the students themselves."

Spencer eyed them. "Would they really be that stupid?"

Reading and Leather exchanged knowing glances. "Let's hope not. Hopefully, they'll be heading to rejoin us so that they can get back in the loop on what's really going on."

"How long will it take them to get to the border?"

"It's not that far. Certainly less than an hour, depending on how hard they want to ride their horses. Knowing them, they won't drive them too hard. I'd guess half an hour."

Leather concurred. "Sounds about right, assuming that's their intention."

"God, I hope it is. Two fewer people to be concerned about would be nice."

"And if the shit hits the fan, two more trained guns for the fight."

Reading glanced over at Leather's small security force standing nearby, geared up and ready to go. He checked his watch. Whatever was going to happen, could be happening within the hour.

Imhotep Residence

Memphis, Old Kingdom

2648 BC

Pounding at the door had Imhotep bolting upright in bed. He glanced over at his wife, lying naked beside him, still sleeping peacefully. He had given her a sedative so she would sleep through what was to come, leaving her last memories of him pleasant ones, of making love one final time and falling asleep in each other's arms.

More hammering at the door then a crashing sound had him rolling out of bed, quickly dressing as footfalls pounded throughout the house, servants, family members, and soldiers shouting.

"Father, it's the pharaonic guard!" called his eldest son. "They say they're here to arrest you!"

Imhotep's stomach churned at the words, and he frowned in dismay that his children would be witness to his arrest. "I'll be there in a moment!" He finished dressing. If he was to be arrested, it would be with dignity. He refused to be humiliated in front of his family and staff.

There was a struggle outside the bedroom door as his sons grappled with those sent to arrest him. Someone was going to get hurt, or worse. He opened the door and stepped out into the hall.

"That's enough!" he snapped.

Everyone froze, including the pharaonic guards, for until this morning, Imhotep was a name to be respected and feared due to his association with the pharaoh. The guards stepped back, as did his sons. Imhotep addressed the senior guard, a man he recognized. "What's happening?"

"I've been sent by High Priest Neper to arrest you."

"Arrest me? For what?"

"For the murder of our pharaoh."

His sons gasped and Imhotep gave a worthy performance, stumbling back against the wall, one hand reaching out for support, the other clutching at his chest. "Djoser is dead? My friend is dead?"

"Yes, sir. His servants were unable to wake him this morning."

"Why wasn't I called?"

"The high priest was there and pronounced him dead, then ordered your arrest."

"But I tried to help him. Everyone saw it."

The guard frowned. "I'm sorry, sir, perhaps it's all a misunderstanding, but you'll have to come with us."

"Of course, of course."

Imhotep turned to his children and smiled at them. "I have no doubt this is simply a misunderstanding, but should I not return, know that I love you all. Take care of your mothers."

259

He placed a hand against his eldest son's cheek. "Especially your mother." He tilted his head toward the closed bedroom door. "The family is now yours, my son."

His son stared at him through watering eyes. "You can count on me, Father. I will take care of them all. And know this." He glared at the guards. "None of us will ever believe the lies about to be told."

Someone cleared their throat behind him and Imhotep turned to see High Priest Neper standing there. Imhotep faced him. If there was any hope of surviving this, it would be now.

"Is it true? Is our pharaoh dead?"

Neper bowed his head. "Yes, he is dead."

"I would like to see him."

Neper regarded him. "Why? So you can confirm your treachery was successful?"

Imhotep rolled his eyes. "What is this nonsense? The guard said you believe I murdered my friend. You were there. I tried to help him. Before I left, he was already feeling better."

"You're a clever man, and if I were not there to witness it, perhaps you would have gotten away with it, but fortunately, I saw everything."

Imhotep's heart pounded. He was certain he had forgotten something. Had Neper spotted it? This could all be a bluff, and what happened next could decide his fate. He sighed heavily. "Listen, my best friend is dead. Our pharaoh is dead. No one wants to discover the truth more than I do. So, let's clear this up. What is it you think you saw?"

"Why don't you show me your bag?"

Imhotep's eyes narrowed. "My bag?"

"Yes, your physician's bag that you brought last night."

"Very well." Imhotep led them to his office and pointed at the table. "There."

Neper stepped over to the table and picked up the cup Imhotep had taken from the palace. He sniffed it then ran his finger inside and licked it. He held up the cup. "Now, why would you take this?"

A shiver ran down Imhotep's spine. "I have no idea. I didn't realize I had until I came home. I suppose I was distracted out of concern for my friend."

"Yet you took the time to thoroughly wash it?"

Imhotep's pulse pounded in his ears. "So?"

"So, why bother? Why not have one of your servants wash it and return it to the palace, or simply return it yourself and hand it to one of the servants to take care of? It's a simple cup of little value. For you to personally wash it suggests you were hiding evidence of what you had put in it."

Imhotep forced another eye roll. "You're obviously not a physician. However, you are a holy man and I assume familiar with how to properly handle medical preparations."

"I'm quite familiar."

"Then you must be aware of how dangerous some of the preparations we create can be. A cup left with residue in it could be taken by someone, perhaps a child. If they then drink from it, it could make them very ill and, depending on what it was, perhaps even kill them." He regarded the old man. "Since you've never lived in a household with children and have instead devoted your life to the gods, you would have no experience in what it's like to have children running around. One must be constantly vigilant."

Neper put the cup down. "A well-thought-out explanation, plausible and at the ready." He opened the bag and peered inside, inspecting the contents. "Interesting."

Imhotep wiped the sweat from his brow. "What?"

"Where's the pouch that you so carefully measured two spoonsful of powder from?"

Imhotep's heart hammered at the question and the realization that it was what he had forgotten about. It was the error in his plan, a plan he had believed was so well thought out, no one would question it. But he hadn't counted on someone with the high priest's knowledge being in the room. Yet despite it being a flaw, it could be easily explained away.

He gestured toward the far wall. "I returned what remained to the shelf."

"Again, a well-thought-out answer. And where is the pouch?"

"I burned it."

Neper cocked an eyebrow. "Now, why would you do that?"

"For the same reason I would clean the cup. It can't be reused because it's contaminated."

"And yet another well-thought-out response." Neper gestured at the wall of wooden containers. "Why don't you show me what you administered to our pharaoh?"

Imhotep retrieved two of the containers, one containing the root meant to settle a patient's stomach, the other, a sedative that would relax the patient and help them sleep. He placed the two containers onto the table, his hands shaking.

Neper leaned over, inspecting the contents, sniffing both, then nodded with satisfaction. "Two very common medicines used by all physicians, even used by myself. Do you not agree?"

"Absolutely. So, you can see I treated our pharaoh with two very common preparations. One to settle his stomach, one to help him sleep. There's no way either of these caused his death. Now can we put this nonsense behind us and find out what actually did kill him?"

"Yes, why don't we?"

Neper dumped out the contents of Imhotep's physician's bag on the table, then began picking up each pouch and sniffing it, setting them aside. He picked up another pouch, sniffed, and smiled. He loosened the drawstring and opened the pouch, peering inside. He held it out for Imhotep to see.

"Higan root used to settle an upset stomach?"

"Yes."

"You administered this last night?"

"Yes." Imhotep tapped one of the containers he had retrieved. "As I already indicated."

Neper continued to go through the pouches and stopped at another one. He peered inside. "Zilot root, used to calm a patient and help them get to sleep."

Imhotep tapped the second container. "Again, as I already indicated."

Neper smiled. "Thus proving your guilt."

Imhotep gulped. What had he forgotten? What could possibly have just been said that proved he had murdered his friend? He peered at Neper. "What are you talking about?"

"You don't see it, do you? You don't see the error you made despite it being right in front of you."

Imhotep's stomach churned. "I don't know what you're talking about." His voice was barely a murmur. This wasn't a bluff. Neper had noticed something, something that still escaped him.

Neper held the two pouches in question in his hand. "It was really a well-thought-out crime, and if I hadn't been there, you would've gotten away with it. But unfortunately for you, someone was in the room who knew what to pay attention to and would know what questions to ask after the fact." He held up the two pouches and pointed at the others sitting on the table. "What do you notice about all these pouches?"

Imhotep shrugged. "I'm not sure what you mean."

"Well, there are ten pouches here and they're all identical."

Imhotep had no idea where he was going with this. "Yes. So?"

"These are all well-worn, all the same size, all similar in color, except where they've been stained by their contents. I wouldn't be surprised if they were all cut from the same skin."

Imhotep was still confused. "They were. They were a gift from my wife many years ago."

"A thoughtful gift from a woman who clearly cares about her husband and takes pride in his work." He waved a finger at the pouches. "Yet interestingly, there's nothing on any of these to indicate what's inside. How do you know what's in them?"

Imhotep smiled slightly at Neper's naiveté. "If you were as familiar as I am, you could tell by the weight, the firmness, and of course the smell."

Neper gestured at the wall housing the scores of containers. "So, you can do the same with all of these?"

"Of course not. But I always carry the same ten preparations in my bag to treat the most common ailments. Anything special I would need after seeing a patient, I come back here, prepare it, then return to administer it."

"So, you always carry the same ten?"

"Yes."

"And if you use up one, what do you do?"

"When I return here, I refill it immediately. Always. You never know when you could be called out again."

"So then, when you left to treat our pharaoh, you were confident you had all ten preparations in your bag that you would most likely need?"

"Yes, of course, any good physician would."

"I agree. So, if that were the case, why did you feel the need to bring a separate pouch of Zilot root? If you always carried it with you and you always made certain you had a healthy supply of it, why bring a second pouch that was different than all the others? Why bring a second pouch and burn it when you returned home?" He pointed at the others. "These were all a gift from your wife, kept for many years. You never burned any of them. Why this one time?"

The blood drained from Imhotep's face and he felt faint. This had been the mistake, the mistake he knew in the back of his mind he had made, but couldn't figure out. It was a mistake that would doom him.

265

Neper stepped closer, staring into his eyes. There was no anger, no malice. If anything, it was compassion. "I know why you did it, and I understand why you did it. And if I were in your position, I would hope I would have been brave enough to do the same thing."

"Yet you condemn me."

"I have no choice. My position dictates my actions."

Imhotep closed his eyes, his shoulders slumping. "At least my sister is safe."

"Yes, there is that."

Imhotep's eyes shot open. "My family. What will you do to my family? They knew nothing of this. I acted entirely alone."

"That is up to them."

"What do you mean?"

"They will be given the option to renounce your name, swearing to never speak it again, and denounce your actions. Those who do will be allowed to continue their lives unmolested, the shame of your actions dying with you. But should they not agree, they will die with you."

"And my estate? Will my family be allowed to keep it?"

"It will be sold, but the proceeds will go to your eldest son. After all, the family of the man who murdered a pharaoh cannot be allowed to live in the estate next to the palace."

It broke his heart to think his family would lose their home, but it was a small price to pay for them not to lose their lives. "I must speak with them to make them understand why they must do what is necessary. Will you permit me that one final favor?"

"Of course."

Imhotep stepped into the hallway, his children gathered, held back by the guards. Neper signaled and the guard stepped back, unleashing a flood of outstretched arms. Imhotep clung to them as everyone sobbed, even his eldest son, his brood no doubt having heard the conversation that had taken place in his office, for the door was open.

He drew a deep breath and steeled for the conversation. As much as he wanted to join in with tears of his own, he couldn't. He was their father, the patriarch of the family, and he was still Imhotep, the kingdom's most respected architect and physician, senior advisor to a pharaoh, and until moments ago, one of the most powerful men in the realm.

He gently extricated himself and his eldest stared at him, blurting out the question they no doubt all wanted the answer to. "Why did you do it, Father? Why did you kill Pharaoh?"

Imhotep glanced over at Neper, who shook his head slightly. The truth couldn't be permitted. "It doesn't matter, just know that I had my reasons and I believed I was doing the right thing. I took no joy in my actions and I felt no malice toward my friend, but what I did had to be done." He took a knee. "The high priest has graciously agreed to let the punishment for my crime stop with me. This is a tremendous thing, and you should all be grateful. Don't blame him, for he is merely doing his job, but part of that agreement means you must forget about me. You must move on with your lives and never speak my name again." He squeezed his eyes shut for a moment before continuing, struggling to maintain control. "And at my burial, you must denounce me and my actions."

"Never!" cried his eldest.

Imhotep rose and took his son's hand. "You must. You're the head of the family now. All I have is now yours. Promise me you'll do what I say, otherwise all of you are doomed."

His son glared at Neper, his fists clenched, shoulders squared. Then he finally sighed, splaying his fingers. "Very well, I shall do as you wish." He glanced at the others. "We'll all do as you wish. It will be our way of honoring your memory."

Imhotep smiled and embraced his son. "Then I die content with the knowledge that my family is in good hands. And never forget that your father, even though you may not speak his name, loved you more than you'll ever know." He turned to his eldest. "Your mother sleeps, and will for some time. Explain to her what has happened and make it clear it's my desire for you all to heed my final wishes, and tell her that my final words were of her and my eternal love for her."

Tears rolled down his son's cheeks. "I shall, Father."

Imhotep embraced each of his children individually, then turned to Neper. "I'm ready."

Yet he wasn't. And as he was escorted out of his own home by the pharaonic guard, he continually reminded himself of why he had done what he had, and how it was the right thing. He had saved his sister and countless others from a similar fate, and if that meant he had to suffer for eternity, then he could accept that.

Though he prayed the gods would forgive him when his fate was put in their hands.

Exploratory Site

Sudan

Present Day

"Got something!" shouted Utkin.

Tankov spun toward the excited shout. "What is it?"

"We found another vehicle!"

Tankov jogged over to join the others and smiled at the top of what appeared to be a transport. He signaled for the team operating the Suck-and-Blow to resume. "Let's go. Clear out the back. I want to see what's inside."

"Yes, sir."

The machine fired up again, the suction hose vacuuming up the sand then spitting it out well behind them. Everyone, including the Sudanese and the captive students, approached, all eager to see what was inside. His two men operating the nozzle cleared out the rear, revealing the tailgate.

269

"That's enough!" shouted Tankov over the roar of the machine, and the motor powered down. He skidded down the edge of the hole created by the vacuum then tore aside the canvas cover and peered inside.

At nothing.

He pulled a flashlight off his belt and shone it inside, certain his eyes must be deceiving him, but they weren't. There were a few discarded pallets, and that was it. It was empty. He stepped back. "Nothing."

Groans from those waiting with bated breath greeted his report. Utkin slid down to join him. "How the hell can there be nothing?"

Tankov gestured for his friend to look for himself. "Nothing but a couple of pallets and a pile of sand."

Utkin scrambled inside and a moment later cursed. "Look at this!"

"What?"

"Come see." Tankov climbed inside and joined Utkin, who pointed up at the canvas cover of the transport. "It's been cut open."

"Are you sure it didn't just tear?"

Utkin dismissed the suggestion. "Too clean. I think they cut it open from the top here, up at the front, then unloaded it."

"Why the hell would they do that?"

Utkin shrugged. "Maybe the back was buried in sand, so they could only get to it from the front, and whatever was inside was too valuable to leave behind."

Tankov didn't like the sound of that. If this transport had been emptied, it meant either the Nazis hadn't been trapped here like they had been told, or the convoy had been discovered long ago and looted, though he suspected the latter wasn't the case. Surely, if the items from

Imhotep's tomb had gone on the black market, he would know, even if it was from decades ago. The collectors of antiquities like this quite often tired of their possessions and sold them to others in exchange for new finds to stimulate the imagination for a few months or years.

He climbed back out, Utkin following, then pointed ahead. "There's nothing in here but there might have been. Let's keep going and see if there's another vehicle."

The machine fired back up as his team repositioned, and he climbed out of the hole, extending a hand and dragging Utkin out.

"What did you find?" asked one of the students.

Tankov decided there was no harm in satisfying their curiosity. "It was empty, just a couple of discarded pallets. But it looks like somebody cut open the roof from the front."

The young man's eyes widened. "So, it might have been unloaded from the front?"

"Yes, that's a possibility."

An excited, whispered conversation between the students began as Colonel Abdeen approached. "I understand it's empty."

"Yes, but there was something in there at some point."

"So then, it might have already been looted?"

"Possibly." Tankov gestured at the sand stretching out in front of them. "This is completely filled in. If it was discovered, it wasn't recent."

"What are you suggesting?"

"I'm suggesting we need to keep looking to see if there are more trucks. They might have just found this one, and the rest are still buried,

271

or they were never trapped here at all, and the rest got away. There's only one way to know for sure, and that's to keep digging."

The colonel tapped his watch. "You have until my troops arrive, then we're leaving. With what happened with the Bedouins, it's too dangerous to stay here."

Tankov frowned but didn't bother arguing with the man. He was right. The sooner they were out of here, the better. And besides, he had a sneaking suspicion there was nothing here to be found.

Egypt/Sudan Border Crossing

Acton hailed Reading and Leather, waiting on the Egyptian side of the border for them. The Sudanese guards had waved them through, merely glancing up at the two riders on horseback wearing Bedouin clothing, the Bedouin in the region usually given free passage across their traditional lands. The Egyptian side was more on the ball, inspecting their passports and visas, then were delighted when the horses were handed over.

"They're all yours," said Acton with a smile.

They walked over to the SUV and hugs and handshakes were exchanged. "Thank God you're all right," said Reading, holding on to Laura a little bit longer.

She smiled up at him and patted his cheek. "It's so good to see you."

"And you. Now, let's get the hell out of here before someone starts asking questions."

They climbed into the SUV and Leather drove them toward their informal observation post. "Do you need to get back to the dig?" he asked.

273

Laura shook her head. "No. I assume you're still set up where we previously discussed?"

"Yes, we've got a direct line of sight on the dig."

"What's going on?" asked Acton. "We've been out of the loop for quite a bit."

"The Russian convoy arrived a while ago, and they've gone to work with that equipment."

"What does it do?" asked Acton.

"It's hard to tell from our position, but it's kicking up an awful lot of dust. Langley says it appears to be some sort of giant vacuum cleaner."

Laura gasped. "Barbarians! That's no way to conduct a dig!"

"Unfortunately, that's not what they're doing." Acton sighed. "They're like the conquistadors. Collect the gold carvings, melt them down, and ship the gold bars home."

Laura punched the back of Reading's seat. "They have to be stopped."

"What may or may not be there is no longer our concern," said Reading. "Our only concern now is the students."

Laura sighed. "You're right, of course. So, what's happening with that?"

"Very little that's good," said Reading. "We've got Sudanese reinforcements, at least fifty men and two helicopters, already en route. They'll be here in less than an hour. We've got your Bedouin tribes gathering and they could be ready to attack around the same time."

"What about a rescue op?"

"Delta is on their way, but from what we've been told, they're going to hold on the Egyptian side and figure out what to do. It's just too dangerous for them to go in with that many people."

"They have to do something." Laura pulled at her hair. "Somebody has to do something."

Acton took her hand and gave it a gentle squeeze. "You know they'll do whatever they can."

"Do we know if it's Bravo Team?"

Reading shook his head. "No, CIA hasn't said, but even if it isn't, you know they'll do everything they can."

Leather brought them to a halt and they all climbed out. Spencer joined them as Leather headed off to his team. Acton gestured at the heavily armed men. "What's going on here?"

"The plan is to cross the border and provide support should it become necessary."

"Good. Count me in."

"Me too," said Laura.

"Me three."

Reading dismissed his son's volunteerism. "Not bloody likely. You're staying right here with me."

"You're not going with them?"

Reading gave him a look. "I'm too old for this shit. Desert combat's a young man's game."

"Which is exactly why I should be going."

"You're a British police officer and you're not trained for this."

Spencer gestured at Acton and Laura. "And they are?"

"You'd be surprised at just what they're trained for."

Acton grinned. "We're killing machines."

Reading grunted. "Just remember, machines can get killed too."

Exploratory Site

Sudan

Tankov frowned as Utkin gave a thumbs-down. They had cleared at least five feet down and found nothing for two good car lengths. The Sudanese column would soon be here, and this was turning into a waste of time. He pointed at a nearby contraption the students had been using when he first arrived. "What is that?"

The young man who appeared to be taking charge stepped forward. "Ground-penetrating radar."

"Do you know how to use it?"

"Yes, sir."

"Then use it." Tankov pointed ahead of the fresh holes dug by his team. "Turn it on and start checking ahead. Let us know if you find anything." The young man nodded and headed for the machine, the others following. Tankov held out a hand, stopping the leader. "And if I catch you lying to me, I'll shoot you."

Eyes bulged and there was a hasty nod.

Tankov let him proceed and gestured at Utkin. "Watch them. As soon as they find something, get the machine in there. We don't have any time to waste."

"Yes, sir."

One of the Sudanese shouted and Tankov turned to see a soldier pointing in the distance at a cloud of dust on the horizon. The question was, was it the Sudanese column coming to escort them to safety, or the Bedouins hellbent on revenge?

Either way, it wasn't good news.

Operations Center 2, CIA Headquarters
Langley, Virginia

Morrison entered the operations center and Leroux pushed to his feet. He was exhausted. He hadn't slept in 36 hours, and right now was fueled by adrenaline and Diet Dr. Pepper.

"Status?"

Leroux indicated the main display. "The Sudanese column is about to arrive. They're about five minutes out."

"What do you think their intentions are?"

"I would've said their plan was to reinforce the dig, but there are indications that the troops already there are prepping to leave."

"They must have gotten wind that the Bedouins were coming."

"Possibly, though communications are so bad in the area, that it's more likely they're assuming they're coming and they don't want to take any chances."

"And what about our Bedouins?"

Leroux indicated the map where three large red circles were shown. "The red circles are three masses of Bedouin fighters. They're all converging to the southeast of the dig site. If they all wait to meet up, it could be an hour before they all converge on the dig. But if the nearest group wants to, they're only fifteen minutes out."

"How many are we talking?"

"The biggest group, which is the closest, is over a hundred men. The other two are about fifty each."

Morrison cursed. "And Delta, have they landed in Egypt yet?"

"No, sir. They changed their plans."

Morrison cocked an eyebrow. "On whose authority?"

"Operational. Dawson said there was no time to execute the original plan if there was any hope to get the students out alive."

"Then where are they?"

Leroux indicated a pulsing green circle. "About to be in the thick of it, sir."

Approaching the Exploratory Site
Sudan

Dawson hopped to the ground and rushed away from the chopper as the rest of his team followed. The Black Hawk lifted off, heading away from the encampment toward a holding position in Egypt where two other Black Hawks were waiting.

He gave the dust a chance to settle then got his bearings and indicated a direction. Langley had informed him that the Russians' machine was operating and it was likely to be very loud, but they were shutting it on and off periodically. He couldn't risk inserting too close to the dig, otherwise, any element of surprise would be eliminated. His thinking was that the Sudanese weren't the danger. It was when the Sudanese mixed with the Bedouins that all hell would break loose. If he could reach them before that, they might be able to negotiate.

He wasn't overly concerned about the numbers they were facing. Sixty or so poorly trained Sudanese soldiers weren't much of a challenge to a dozen highly trained Special Forces. His men could take out half the

Sudanese in the first five seconds if they had the element of surprise, the bulk of what remained in the next ten.

It was the Russians that were more of a concern. If they had the element of surprise, his men could engage the Russians first in the opening few seconds, but in doing so, any that survived would be his enemy. And right now, he wasn't certain if they were. These were opportunists. Profiteers. They weren't there for political reasons. And if he just targeted the Sudanese, then an experienced commander like Tankov would recognize that and might simply order his men to take cover and only fire if fired upon. Apparently, Leroux had a conversation with the man and made it crystal clear what was expected of him when it came to the lives of the students. Hopefully, it had an effect.

Red joined him as they jogged. "What's the plan, BD?"

Dawson grunted. "Still working on it."

"Cutting it a little close, aren't we?"

"As close as the shave on your head?"

Red lifted his cap and ran his hand over his bald scalp. "How about we try not to cut it that close? The men are getting a little antsy."

Dawson glanced back at the others. "They seem fine."

Red swatted him. "Okay, *I'm* getting antsy."

Dawson laughed. "Then shut the hell up so I can think."

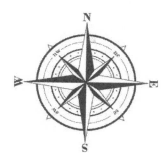

Exploratory Site

Sudan

Tankov cursed as Utkin shook his head, the ground-penetrating radar finding nothing yet again. He had the Suck-and-Blow machine trailing the radar, just in case it was wrong, but so far they had come up with nothing beyond one car with a body in it and an empty transport. There was nothing else. For all he knew, fifty feet beyond where they were, there could be a dozen vehicles buried in the sand. They would never know if they weren't given the time to properly look.

Colonel Abdeen approached. "It's time to leave. The escort helicopters have reported a group of Bedouins are on their way here. Less than ten minutes out. We have to leave now."

Tankov cursed. "When can we return?"

Abdeen flicked a wrist at the unsuccessful effort. "Why bother? There's nothing here."

Tankov disagreed. "We found two vehicles. Obviously there is something here. We just haven't found anything of value yet."

"When things settle down, we can discuss a return, but until then, we have to leave the area while we still can."

"Fine. But it's going to take time to pack up the equipment."

"You have five minutes."

Tankov cursed and started barking orders, his men leaping into action as they quickly packed up the Suck-and-Blow machine. There was no way in hell he wanted to abandon it in the desert when there was no payday at the end of it. It was an expensive piece of equipment that could be used elsewhere.

The Sudanese captain ordered the students to stop their work then had them line up on the edge of one of the empty holes dug by the machine.

He tensed. This was it. The Sudanese were going to execute the students and use the hole to bury the bodies. The CIA hadn't been bluffing. The Bedouins were coming and the plan all along had been to kill the students. Now the question was, what was the plan for his men?" He waved Utkin over.

"What's up?"

"I'm not sure, but I think the Sudanese are about to execute the students."

"So do I. Are we going to let that happen?"

Tankov scanned the area. The Sudanese were packing up, readying to head out, but none of their troops were in their transports. They were all on the ground, which made no sense if they were leaving within a few minutes. "There's a theory going around that the Sudanese might be planning on killing the students *and* us."

Utkin eyed him. "Going around, huh?"

Tankov tapped his skull. "In my head."

"Well, that's not good."

"No, it isn't."

"What are we going to do about it?"

"I've been assured by somebody in Washington, or more likely, Langley, that if anything happens to the students, Red Notices will be issued on all of us."

Utkin frowned. "Well, if that's the case, there's not much point in surviving today, is there?"

"No."

"What do you want us to do?"

"Spread the word to the others to be ready, and make sure everyone's got a weapon. The guys packing up only have their sidearms."

"Roger that."

Tankov casually strolled over to the students, all of them terrified. They had obviously clued into what was happening.

"Are you going to kill us?" asked one of the women being held by the young man in charge.

He noticed matching wedding bands. "*I'm* not going to kill you." His eyes darted toward the Sudanese to his left. "But I'm pretty sure they are."

"I fail to see the difference."

"No, I suppose you wouldn't from your side of the equation." He lowered his voice. "If you hear me yell, or you hear a shot, jump into the hole. Don't hesitate, just jump in." He didn't wait for an

285

acknowledgment. He simply walked away, exchanging looks with a couple of his men, Utkin having updated everybody over their comms as to what was going on.

The engine of the Suck-and-Blow fired up and one of his men backed it up toward the flatbed that had brought it here, guided by Utkin. Everyone else was now armed and spread out, no two men clumped together. He surveyed the area, searching for the colonel since he would be the one giving the order, but he didn't spot him at first. The helicopter that had brought them powered up and Tankov cursed.

The coward was going to give the order from the air.

That meant it would be the captain giving it on the ground. He spotted the bastard crouching behind a transport, a radio pressed to his ear as the chopper lifted off.

Tankov activated his comms. "As soon as I open fire, take as many of them out as you can. Watch your arcs and whatever you do, don't hit those students."

The helicopter banked south toward Khartoum and the captain's radio squawked. He stood and Tankov raised his weapon, putting two rounds in the man's chest. "Get in the hole!"

Egypt/Sudan Border

Gunfire rattled across the desert and Acton cursed. "What do you think?" he asked Leather, whose ear was more expert than his.

"AKs and HKs. It's not Delta."

"Shit."

"They could be executing the students!" Laura sprinted across the border and Acton cursed again.

"Let's go!" He raced after her, Leather's team on their heels, sprinting toward the fray. He caught up to Laura as the gunfire grew in intensity. "You remember the plan?"

"Yes."

He frowned. He had no doubt she remembered the plan. The question was, would she follow it? She felt personally responsible for her students and he understood that. He did as well. But getting herself killed wouldn't save them.

He spotted the relay he had planted earlier and glanced over at Leather. "How close do we need to get?"

"A hell of a lot closer than this if we're going to be useful."

Acton frowned as what he had suspected was confirmed. "You take the lead. Get us as close as you think we need to be."

"Roger that." Leather took off ahead of them when a new gun entered the battle.

Laura pointed ahead at a gunship as it opened fire. "Oh no! They're going to kill them all!"

Exploratory Site

Sudan

Dawson and the others sprinted ahead as he activated his comms. "Control, Zero-One. Sit rep, over."

Leroux immediately replied. "Zero-One, Control. It looks like the Russians have engaged the Sudanese, over."

Dawson's eyebrows shot up as he exchanged a surprised glance with Red. "Can you repeat that, Control? Did you say the Russians have engaged the Sudanese?"

"Affirmative, Zero-One."

"Status on the students?"

"All five appear to be taking cover in a hole that was dug earlier. We believe at the moment they're all alive."

"Am I hearing a gunship?"

"Affirmative. One gunship is on the scene. A second will be there inside of three minutes."

Dawson cursed. "What about those Bedouins?"

"Three minutes out as well. One hundred-plus, all appear to be armed with AK variants."

Dawson shook his head. There were too many guns here, but things had changed. The Russians were now the enemy of the Sudanese, and the old adage still stood.

The enemy of my enemy is my friend.

Mitchell draped himself over Jenny. He was the most senior of the five. He ran the dig when Laura wasn't there. He was in charge. He was responsible for the others. Yet how could he be? He was terrified, shaking like a leaf, unable to put together a coherent thought. The gunfire surrounding them was intense. The moment the Russian had shouted at them to get in the hole, he had spread out his arms and pushed everyone he could reach inside, but that was only Jenny and Valdez.

He squeezed his eyes shut and thought back to the training Leather and his team had been providing over the past several years. Beyond weapons and self-defense, survival techniques had been drilled into them, including what to do in exactly a situation like this.

Leather's words echoed in his head. "It's all right to be scared shitless, as long as you don't lose control. Bravery isn't an absence of fear. It's pushing forward despite it."

Mitchell sucked in a breath through his nose and held it, then slowly exhaled through his mouth, repeating the process several times as he steadied his nerves. "Are you all right?" he asked Jenny, and she nodded.

"I think so. You?"

"I think so." He twisted his head to see Valdez beside him. "Are you all right?"

Valdez's eyes bulged with fear. "Yes, I think so."

"Cossio, Johnson, you two all right?"

Cossio groaned from behind him. "I think I broke my arm, but I'll live."

"Johnson, you all right?" There was no response and Mitchell's heart raced even faster. He pushed up on his elbows, careful to keep his head low. Valdez was lying on his back behind them, and Cossio was leaning against the edge of the hole, gripping her arm. He spotted Johnson face down in the dirt and gasped. He scrambled over to him and grabbed him by the shoulder, flipping him onto his back. The young man stared up at him blankly, gripped by terror. Mitchell put a hand on Johnson's chest and felt it rise. He was breathing. He was just dominated by fear.

Valdez joined him. "What's wrong with him? Is he okay?"

"He's fine. He's just scared."

Valdez cursed. "He was involved in a school shooting about ten years ago. A lot of people died."

Mitchell shook his head. He couldn't understand why America failed to see they were the only country in the world with this problem, yet allowed themselves to be dominated by the extremes on either side of the argument. This poor man was suffering from PTSD, still traumatized by what no child should ever have to go through, and almost no child outside of America in the democratic world ever had to worry about.

He took Johnson by the hand and squeezed it, staring into his eyes. "You're going to be all right. This'll be over soon. Just stay down and

291

we'll protect you." It was a hollow promise, but Johnson's eyes flickered, refocusing on Mitchell's. Mitchell smiled at him. "You just stay right where you are. This'll be over soon." He turned to Valdez. "He's your friend. Just talk to him and keep your head down."

Valdez nodded, taking Johnson's hand from Mitchell. Mitchell scurried over to Cossio, now being tended to by Jenny. "How's her arm?"

"Looks like a clean break."

"It hurts like a mother," winced Cossio.

"I can imagine." Mitchell searched for anything they could use as a splint but found nothing. "You're going to have to wait. When this is over, we'll get a splint on that. But for now, just try to keep it as still as possible."

Cossio grimaced. "Anybody happen to have some Kentucky bourbon on them? It would really help with the pain."

Jenny laughed at the young woman. "I never pictured you as a bourbon drinker."

"Never had it in my entire life, but I've always imagined it to be really strong and painful to drink, exactly what I need right now."

"I wish I could help you. The best I can do is break your leg then you won't feel your arm."

Cossio laughed then winced. "Okay, don't make me laugh."

Jenny patted the woman's leg. "All right, no more jokes." She turned to Mitchell, the gunfire continuing unabated, a heavy weapon joining in. "What the hell is that?"

"I think it's a helicopter."

Jenny's eyes closed briefly as they all realized the implication of this new development. While the Russians might be well-trained and capable, there was no way they could stand up to a helicopter with guns. And once the Russians, who were now their protectors, were killed, everything he had just told Johnson would become a lie.

None of them were making it out of this alive.

Dawson hit the ground and the others did the same on either side of him. He pointed at the chopper pouring lead on the encampment. "Atlas, take it out of my sky."

Niner helped Atlas set up the FIM-92A Stinger portable surface-to-air missile system, and the big man took a knee, aiming the device at the chopper. "I've got tone! Firing!" warned Atlas, then he held in the trigger, the shoulder-launched missile erupting from the weapon system a few seconds later, the whoosh of its propellant rapidly fading as it raced toward the chopper. The pilot spotted it and jerked the stick, banking them hard away from the incoming ordnance, but the missile had already locked onto the heat from the engine. The missile slammed into the exposed belly of the helicopter and smoke billowed from it as it collapsed to the ground, exploding on impact.

Dawson rose. "Good job. Keep your eyes open. There could be two more out there. If you see them, just make sure it's not a friendly then take them out. Don't wait for my order."

"Yes, Sergeant Major," echoed Niner and Atlas as Atlas re-slung his gear.

The sound of HKs became more intense, the preferred weapon of the Russians re-engaging now that the chopper had been taken out of the equation. Dawson ordered his men to split up so they could take the objective from three sides. He continued forward with Niner, Atlas, and Spock as Red broke right and Jimmy left with the rest of the team.

Dawson raised his M4 and advanced rapidly, the others spreading out so they didn't make a juicy target. The Russians were pinned down around a flatbed with a large piece of equipment on the back. At least two of them were either dead or wounded, but over a dozen Sudanese were down.

"Control, Zero-One, where the hell are those students?"

"On your two o'clock. They're in a hole that's about ten feet deep."

Dawson spotted it, though couldn't see anyone inside from this angle. He indicated the hole to the others. "The students are in there. Atlas, Niner, get in there, check them out. Get them ready to travel. Spock, you're with me. Take out any Sudanese that you can." He activated his comms. "Bravo Team, Zero-One, take out the Sudanese at will. Leave the Russians alone for now, over."

Red and Jimmy acknowledged and Dawson charged forward. "Friendlies approaching from the south!" he shouted, several of the Russians turning.

He recognized Tankov from their last encounter and the man shouted in Russian, "Don't shoot the Americans!"

Dawson rushed toward their position, taking disciplined shots, each one removing an enemy from the equation as Spock did the same beside him. Something to his right caught his eye. Dust billowing on the horizon.

Is that a sandstorm?

Niner dove into the hole, rolling to the bottom, then braced himself as the massive Atlas hit him full force. He grunted then shoved the big man off him and gave him a look. "I think you did that on purpose."

"Of course I did that on purpose."

Niner patted the big man's cheek. "Next time I'll let you linger."

Atlas groaned as he rolled to a knee. "Who's in charge?"

A young man raised his hand unconvincingly. "I am. Terrence Mitchell."

Niner recognized him. "Okay, Terrence, we're friendlies. US Special Forces. What's the situation?"

Mitchell drew a fortifying breath. "We have one with a broken arm that we have no way to treat." The young man indicated someone lying on the ground. "And he's in shock. Possibly PTSD. He was involved in a school shooting when he was younger. His name is Steve Johnson."

Niner cursed. He had seen PTSD among men and women he had served with. In the old days, they used to call it shell-shocked and it was treated like a coward's disease. Those suffering from it were shunned, those consumed by it desperate to keep that fact a secret, never speaking of what they had gone through for fear of being labeled a coward. Today, there was still a stigma, but at least now it was understood, and those with the courage to come forward and admit they were hurting could get treatment, and those like him who truly understood the horrors of combat, more understanding than they used to be.

He crawled over to the young man and smiled. "Hey, buddy, don't you worry about a thing. The cavalry has arrived. We're going to get you out of here. But for now, I want you to lie right where you are, okay? Just take it easy. Breathe in and out, nice and slow, nice and deep. That big explosion you heard a few minutes ago, that was the helicopter. We took it out and now with our arrival, the odds have evened up quite a bit, so you're going to be all right. When you're ready, sit up and let us know, okay?"

Johnson said nothing, though had stared him in the eyes the entire time. Niner patted the young man's shoulder then joined Atlas who was tending to the broken arm. "How does it look?"

Atlas shrugged. "What am I, an x-ray machine? Haven't a clue. Painful?"

"The only thing you're good at is being eye candy." Niner jerked a thumb up toward the top of the hole. "Get some eyes up there. Make sure we're not about to be overrun. I'll deal with this." Atlas scrambled up the side as Niner retrieved his med kit. He smiled at the wounded woman. "What's your name, darling?"

"Norma."

"I knew a Norma once. She broke my heart. Are you going to break my heart?"

Norma giggled. "Only if you hurt me."

Niner clasped his chest. "Then, darling, you're going to break my heart, because this is going to hurt like a mofo."

"Do you have any bourbon?"

Niner laughed. "I wish I did." He quickly went to work, cutting away the sleeve of her shirt and inspecting the arm. "This is where you break my heart. Ready?"

She nodded and he set the bone, the poor girl screaming out in agony. He fit the splint in place then secured it. He gently placed her arm on her chest. "Okay, the worst of it's over. Any pain from now on will be a lot less than what you just went through."

"If you say so."

"Would I lie to you?"

"I don't know. I'm not your biggest fan at the moment."

He laughed. "I like you. You've got lady balls. Now, I can give you painkillers. I've got pills that will start working in about twenty minutes, and a needle that will work in seconds. The needle affects the old noggin'"—he tapped her forehead—"so I'd advise against it just in case you need to think on your feet. If you don't think you can take the pain, I'll give you the needle and we'll carry you out. Your choice."

"No needles, but load me up with the pills, and next time, lie to me and tell me they'll work in five minutes so that I'll at least have the placebo effect."

He grinned. "I promise. But if there is a next time, I highly suggest you switch careers, because this one's obviously bad luck."

Atlas rolled down the side of the hole, this time avoiding taking out those below.

"Status?"

"We've got a group of about a dozen that are trying to flank the Russian position. They're approaching this hole."

"Any sign they know we're in it?"

Mitchell grunted. "Oh, they know. Those bastards were all standing around while we were lined up in front of it waiting to be shot. This was supposed to be our grave."

Niner frowned as he handed the painkillers to Mitchell, along with a canteen. "Have her take these." He scrambled up the side of the hole, keeping his head down. Atlas joined him and pointed.

"Right there. Three o'clock."

Niner turned and cursed as the last of the squad dropped into a depression and out of sight, one of them making eye contact with him. "Well, they know we're here."

"Grenades?" suggested Atlas.

"Grenades."

Dawson took up position behind the wheel of a transport as he opened fire on a nearby light armored vehicle with a .50 cal. He glanced over at the Russians. "What's your status?"

Tankov repositioned, and between shots, filled him in. "I've got one dead, two wounded, and we're running low on ammo. We're not equipped for a sustained battle."

Dawson's comms squawked in his ear. "Zero-One, Control, those Bedouins are sixty seconds out, over."

"Copy that, Control. What are they doing, over?"

"It looks like they're spreading out. They're going to try to surround the whole area."

"Copy that. Zero-One, out. Bravo Team, Zero-One. We've got less than sixty seconds before the Bedouins get here, and it looks like they aim to surround us."

Explosions erupted to his right as grenades detonated and their victims cried out in agony and terror. He spotted Niner and Atlas lobbing another pair, and breathed a sigh of relief that it wasn't any of his men or the students that had just been killed.

"One-One, Zero-One, what's your status, over."

Niner replied. "I've got one with a broken arm, one in shock. The other three are mobile."

"Can the one with the broken arm run?"

"Should be able to with a little help."

"All right. We're getting out of here and we're getting out of here now. Get Atlas to sling the shock victim over his shoulder if necessary. Get the healthy students to help the one with the broken arm, and be prepared to head directly north the moment I give the word, over."

"Roger that. Let us know when you're ready."

The rotors of another helicopter pounded at the air as it approached, and Dawson cursed.

"Zero-One, Control. We've got that second gunship returning."

"What's it doing?"

"It looks like they're setting up between the main Sudanese position and the Bedouins."

299

Gunfire erupted from the chopper and Dawson instinctively crouched. "Who are they firing on?"

"The Bedouins."

"And what's their reaction?"

"They're splitting off south."

Dawson smiled. "Does that mean the north is clear except for the Sudanese?"

"Yes."

"Copy that. Let's send in the choppers. We'll meet them on the Egyptian side of the border."

"Roger that, Zero-One, good luck."

"From your lips to God's ears. Zero-One, out."

Now, let's see whose side God's truly on.

He eyed the large piece of Russian equipment on the flatbed and smiled at the heavens.

Good idea.

Leather hit the ground just ahead and Acton thanked God when Laura dropped beside him. He was afraid he was going to have to push her to the ground himself, but the situation had changed since they had started running toward the gunfire. M4s had joined the battle, as had something capable of shooting a helicopter out of the sky. It had to mean Delta was on the scene.

The second helicopter that had just arrived was focusing on the dust cloud to the east that had to be the Bedouins arriving for their revenge. Acton peered through his binoculars and gasped at the carnage and chaos. At least a couple dozen Sudanese were down and gunfire raged in every direction. The Russians appeared to be pinned near a flatbed with their large sand removal machine, but he couldn't see the students. He spotted four men to the right, dressed in special ops gear. "I think I've got four Delta guys on the right."

"Confirmed. There's four more on the left as well," said Leather.

"Let me look." Acton handed the binoculars over to Laura. She peered through them then handed them back. "What's going on with that flatbed?"

Acton looked and his eyes narrowed as one of the Russians jumped behind the wheel of the sand remover. "What the hell is he doing?"

"Bravo Team, Zero-One, concentrate all fire on the western flank. I want that side cleared, then when I give the word, converge on the giant vacuum cleaner, over."

The acknowledgments came in through his headset as the large vacuum rolled off the back of the flatbed then turned, facing north. Gunfire from Red and Jimmy's teams switched focus as he and Spock continued to keep the heads down of the other Sudanese. He shouted at Tankov, pointing to their western flank. "Have your men concentrate their fire over there!"

Tankov acknowledged him with a nod, passing on the order to his men. Soon over a dozen weapons were focused on the area, mowing down from three directions the Sudanese that remained. Two of the Russians scrambled to set up the front hose on a remote-controlled manipulator arm that extended from the front of the machine. The motor for the vacuum fired up and sand began spitting out the back as the two men repositioned the rear hose, hooking it into a cradle, launching the sand directly into the air.

Dawson activated his comms. "One-One, Zero-One, are you ready?"

"As ready as we'll ever be."

"Then get ready on my mark!"

Acton stared at the scene ahead. Sand was blowing into the air, creating a dust cloud, obscuring everything for fifty feet around the Russian machine. He smiled. It was brilliant.

Leather turned to them. "This is it. They're going to use that as cover, and it looks like they're going to try to come straight toward us. Concentrate your fire on the Sudanese positions, but if you can't see, don't shoot. It's going to be hard to pick out friend from foe, so only take a shot if you're absolutely positive."

"What about that chopper?" asked Laura, pointing as it banked away from the incoming Bedouins, the pilot obviously taking notice of what the Russians were doing.

Leather cursed. "All right, new target. Let's try to take out that chopper."

Acton took aim as the helicopter swept toward the battle then fired, praying to God for a miracle.

Atlas hauled Johnson to his feet. The young man gasped, blinking rapidly. "Are you okay, kid?"

Johnson nodded. "Yeah. Yeah, I think so," he said, sounding surprised.

"Good man!" Atlas jabbed his ass cheek with a finger. "You stick to my six, okay, and we'll get out of here just fine."

Niner pointed at Mitchell and Jenny kneeling nearby with Cossio. "It's up to you two to get her out of the hole. Atlas and I will be providing cover fire if necessary, but we're not going to try to draw any attention to us unless we have to. Got it?"

"Got it," acknowledged Mitchell, Jenny giving a frightened nod.

Dawson's voice came in over the comms. "One-One, Zero-One. Go, go, go!"

"This is it!" Niner scrambled up the side of the hole and dropped, lying prone on the ground, scanning the area. "We're clear!"

Atlas joined him then reached inside, hauling Johnson out then Valdez, pushing them to the ground. Mitchell and Jenny emerged a moment later with Cossio, tears streaming down her face as she gripped her arm but bore the pain. Niner continued to scan for any of the hostiles noticing them, but for the moment, everyone's attention appeared focused on the Russian machine spewing sand into the air.

Niner took a knee and pointed at the vehicle. "That's our destination. We're going to run over there, and unless I tell you to hit the ground, you just keep running no matter what you see or hear. You're going to go for the left side of the vehicle, away from all those guns over there, and then you're going to use it as cover. Try to get near the wheels. Understood?"

Heads bobbed around him.

"Good. Let's go!" He pushed to his feet and led the way, his weapon trained on the Sudanese soldiers massed ahead and to the right. The students followed, Jenny and Mitchell helping Cossio as Atlas brought up the rear with Johnson and Valdez using the big man as cover. Niner activated his comms. "Friendlies approaching whatever the hell we're calling that thing from the south, over."

Dawson acknowledged and waved at them.

Niner picked up the pace, doing a shoulder check to make sure the others were keeping up, and slowed slightly as he saw Cossio couldn't maintain the pace with the pain. One of the Sudanese shouted, pointing in their direction. Niner cursed and took him out, then switched to full auto, pouring bursts of lead at the enemy position. "Let's go, people!"

Egypt/Sudan Border

Reading watched helplessly through the binoculars at the battle raging only a couple of miles away. He could see Acton and the others had engaged the helicopter, and for the moment had distracted the crew enough that they were no longer directing fire on the Russian machine and those using it as cover, but instead were banking toward his friend's position.

"If that helicopter—"

"I know, I know," he said, stopping Spencer from speaking the words.

The gunfire from Acton's position increased dramatically and he noticed they were no longer prone. Everyone was on their knees as the helicopter neared, some standing. Muzzle flashes from the chopper had him wincing and he kept focused on Acton and Laura. Acton dove to his left then regained his knee, opening fire once again, but the helicopter continued its relentless approach.

His friends were about to die.

305

Exploratory Site

Sudan

Niner made the vehicle first, fitting his goggles in place, the sand intense. He reached out and pulled the others to safety as they arrived at the left side of the machine and the cover it provided.

Dawson slapped him on the back. "Good job." He pointed ahead. "Now take out that damn chopper!"

"You got it, boss." Niner raced ahead with Atlas, through the dust storm created by the machine, then broke through, spotting the chopper ahead, banking to the north, its guns blazing.

"Who the hell are they firing on?" He cursed as he realized who it must be. The professors were supposed to be to the north on the Egyptian side of the border, and knowing them, they would be heading toward the danger, not away from it. They must have engaged the helicopter in an attempt to distract it.

He helped Atlas prep the Stinger, the big man having already reloaded it earlier in their makeshift foxhole. "You ready?"

Atlas gave a thumbs-up. "Ready." He dropped to a knee, steadying his aim, and fired. The missile raced from the launcher, the distinctive sound lost to the roar of the machine behind them, and Niner struggled to keep an eye on the weapon as the blowing sand increased around them. He pushed to his feet and rushed ahead as Atlas reloaded for another shot, but it wasn't necessary. The missile streaked toward its target and slammed into the tail rotor. The chopper spun out of control, hurtling into the ground, fire erupting as the remaining fuel ignited, setting off the ordnance inside.

Dawson's voice came in over the comms. "Good job, One-One and Zero-Seven. Control, Zero-One, do we have anything in the air that's a threat, over?"

"Negative, Zero-One. Nothing in the area," replied Leroux.

"Copy that. One-One, Zero-One, get your asses back under cover, over."

Niner spun around. "Roger that, Zero-One. Repositioning now."

Acton and the others cheered as the helicopter fell out of the sky, exploding a few moments after impact. The Russian machine was slowly approaching, sand still obscuring everything around it, the smoke from the engulfed chopper adding to the reduced visibility. He peered ahead but had no targets.

Leather dropped back to a knee, having been on his feet pouring lead on the chopper. "Everyone hold your fire. We can't see anything through this."

"Should we move in closer?" asked Laura.

"Negative. We hold here, and when they reach us, we provide cover if necessary." He pointed to the east. "But something tells me the Sudanese are going to have their hands full."

Acton peered through the binoculars at the scores of riders on camelback and horseback racing toward the fight. It was a sight to behold, and he wished them well, but he just prayed they arrived too late to interfere with the escape now underway.

The gunfire on them dwindled, though Dawson could still hear the weapons rattling from the Sudanese positions, along with the thundering of hundreds of hooves pounding on the sand as the Bedouins approached. The Sudanese had no doubt taken notice, realizing that those escaping were no longer the threat.

"Hold your fire!" he shouted, and his team's weapons silenced, but the Russians continued to shoot.

He smacked Tankov nearby. "Order your men to cease fire."

"Why the hell would I do that?"

"Because as long as we're a threat, they'll keep shooting at us. If we leave them alone, they'll focus on those Bedouins."

Tankov frowned at him then activated his comms, ordering his men to hold their fire. The Russian weapons fell silent and the remaining Sudanese quickly redirected their attention to the real threat.

Dawson tapped the massive machine. "Can this thing go any faster?"

"Not when the vacuum's operational."

He turned to Niner. "Get the students and the wounded onto this thing."

"Yes, Sergeant Major."

Dawson turned to Tankov. "As soon as everybody's on board, tell your driver to shut off that thing and get moving. The rest of us will hoof it out."

Tankov said nothing but scrambled up the side, opening the driver's side door. Dawson activated his comms. "Control, Zero-One. We're going to make a break for it. Status on those choppers?"

"They're just landing now, approximately two klicks north of your current position."

"Copy that. Keep an eye on our six. Let us know if anything's approaching or if anybody decides to pay attention to us, especially those Bedouins. I don't want to open fire on them, but if I have to, I have to."

"Understood, Zero-One. ROEs allow you to engage if engaged. We'll keep an eye on things for you."

"Copy that, Zero-One, out."

"Everyone's on board!" reported Niner and Dawson reached up and slapped Tankov on the leg, giving him a thumbs-up.

"We're good to go!"

Tankov nodded and leaned into the cab. The vacuum shut down and the engine of the behemoth roared as it jerked ahead, slowly picking up speed. The dust settled around them and within seconds they were staring at desert and blue skies, the Bedouins to the east plainly visible as they raced toward them, the Sudanese behind them, clear as day.

Meaning his people were completely exposed.

This could turn south in a hurry.

Laura rose and waved, and Leather snapped at her. "Get down!"

She dropped to a knee and looked at her head of security. "Why? What's wrong?"

"Right now, the Sudanese probably don't know we're involved, and we need to keep it that way. Let's just let our people reach us and then we'll fall back with them. Keep an eye on the Sudanese positions, but only open fire if they engage our people. I think we're going to be all right, though." He gestured at the Bedouins about to converge on the Sudanese position. "Something tells me they're going to have their hands full."

Heavy gunfire from both sides echoed across the desert sands, the screams of beast and man horrifying. The Russian vehicle was rumbling toward them now at a good clip, and Acton peered through the binoculars, spotting Mitchell and his wife clinging to the side along with the three American students. He recognized Atlas' massive frame and a smile spread with the knowledge it was Bravo Team here to save the day.

He handed the binoculars to Laura. "All of our people are safe thanks to some friends of ours."

Her face brightened and she peered through the glasses, her shoulders slumping in relief. "Thank God!"

Leather rose as the vehicle approached. He waved. "Friendlies ahead!"

Dawson raised a hand, waving at them. "Acknowledged! Friendlies ahead!" he shouted to the others.

The machine rumbled past them and Acton shook Dawson's hand and Laura gave him a quick hug before breaking off to check on her students.

"Fancy meeting you guys here."

Niner grinned as he joined them. "We just happened to be in the area doing a little sightseeing."

They joined the Russians and Bravo Team as they jogged toward the border, ignoring the melee behind them as the Bedouins descended upon the vastly outnumbered Sudanese soldiers. Three helicopters were on the ground near Reading's position, his friend waving at them, urging them on.

"What do you think has him so excited?" asked Acton.

Dawson jerked a thumb over his shoulder at the battle behind them. "My guess is he's worried that as soon as the Bedouins finish up with the Sudanese, they're going to redirect their attention on us."

Acton cursed. "I hadn't thought of that. We're not their enemy."

"We have twelve Russians with us. When they discover the Russians aren't among the bodies, they're coming for them." Dawson turned. "All right, everybody. As soon as we get to the border, everybody gets in those choppers as quickly as possible. We need to vacate this area before the Bedouins finish up with the Sudanese and come for our Russian guests."

The Russian leader eyed Dawson. "You expect us to get on an American military helicopter?"

"It's either that or die what I'm guessing will be pretty gruesome deaths once the Bedouins get their hands on you."

Tankov frowned. "What do you intend to do with us?"

311

"He saved our lives, sir," said Mitchell, still gripping the side of the Russian vehicle. "If it wasn't for him and his men, we'd be dead."

Jenny backed him up. "It's true. They had us lined up. They were going to shoot us."

Acton shrugged. "What do your orders say?"

"The only orders I have concerning the Russians is to shoot them if they shoot at me."

"Did they shoot at you?"

"No."

"Then I guess it's up to you."

They approached the helicopters and Dawson pointed to the one on the far left. "Russians, get in that chopper. Tell the pilot to drop you off outside of Aswan. I'm sure you can find a ride from there."

Tankov smiled and extended a hand, and Dawson shook it. "Thank you, Sergeant Major. Once again you've proven to be an honorable man."

Dawson frowned. "Yes, it's one of my worst traits. Just remember the next time we encounter each other what I did for you today."

Tankov chuckled. "It won't be forgotten. Unless of course you shoot first."

Dawson held a finger to his ear then cursed, turning toward the battle behind them, the gunfire having stopped. "All right, everybody on the choppers now! They're coming this way!" His men helped the students off the transport, the Russians assisting their own, then everyone raced toward the helicopters.

Acton pointed, shouting at Reading and Spencer. "Get on the choppers! Get on the choppers!"

Spencer stared at him blankly but Reading didn't hesitate, grabbing his son by the arm and heading for the nearest helicopter, the one to the far left.

"No, one of the other ones!" shouted Acton, but it was too late. The helicopters were too loud and his friend couldn't hear him.

Dawson laughed. "How does Hugh feel about Russians?"

"How do you think he feels?"

"Don't worry. We'll get them back to you soon enough."

They poured across the road that marked the Egyptian side of the border as the pounding of hooves rapidly approached. The Russians streamed onto their chopper, Reading and Spencer already aboard. The students, Leather's team, and Acton and Laura boarded the second chopper, while Delta jumped into the third. All three lifted off as the Bedouins rapidly closed the gap, un-aimed gunfire filling the air, a few pings off the fuselage heard as the pilots banked away, heading north, deeper into Egypt before banking to the east and the Red Sea.

Acton breathed a sigh of relief as the pilot announced the all-clear, then he asked the question he was dying to get an answer to. "So, what did you find?"

Mitchell frowned. "Nothing. Just one car with a body, and an empty transport. There was nothing else there for at least fifty meters."

Laura sighed, her head falling back against the fuselage as she closed her eyes. "Then all of this was for nothing. So many dead for nothing. It's all my fault."

Jenny shook her head. "No, ma'am, this isn't your fault at all. This is Rachel's fault. If she hadn't violated our trust, the Russians would have never been there, the second group of Sudanese would never have arrived with their corrupt colonel, and the Bedouins would have never been out for revenge. This is all her fault, and I intend to let her know, then maybe she'll understand the consequences of her actions."

The words were harsh, though true. It certainly wasn't Laura's fault, though to lay the blame entirely on a naïve Gen Z influencer was perhaps misguided. It was her fault, though she didn't force the Russians to act on what they had discovered because of her, she hadn't forced the Bedouins to attack nor to seek revenge for that failed attack, and she hadn't forced a corrupt colonel to order the deaths of the students. There was plenty of blame to go around, though there would be nothing to stop Jenny from reading the riot act to an irresponsible social media junkie who had been the catalyst for at least a hundred deaths.

University College London Dig Site
Lower Nubia, Egypt

Reading had spent about sixty seconds expressing how overjoyed he was to see everyone safe, then the next ten minutes bitching about being stuck on a helicopter with a dozen Russians. The man was not a fan. The reunion on the USS Dwight D. Eisenhower had been brief, however. Pleasantries were exchanged with Delta before they were redeployed, and a helicopter had returned everyone else to Laura's dig site in Egypt in dramatic fashion, though Cossio and Johnson had opted for flights home. Acton suspected Cossio would return after she healed up, but he had a feeling they had seen the last of Johnson, the poor kid traumatized twice in his young life.

Jenny never got a chance to give Rachel a piece of her mind. The kid had sneaked into Laura's tent and sent an email to her father asking to be picked up immediately, and had left for Cairo the day before. Laura had said good riddance, though not before confirming the girl had made it onto her plane and was no longer her responsibility, then declared the dig's charter would be renegotiated to make certain no one could ever be forced upon her again.

But for now, Acton didn't want to think about such things. Instead, he sipped on his ice-cold beer with Laura, Reading, and Spencer in the air-conditioned RV. "This is the life," he said.

Reading shrugged. "Yes, which can be had in London every day, all day."

Acton jerked his head at the desert outside. "Sometimes you need to experience that to appreciate what you truly have."

Reading raised his beer, room temperature, something Acton just couldn't understand. "I'll give you that. I'm just glad none of our people were seriously hurt."

Laura frowned. "None of our people, but the Bedouins and the Sudanese paid a heavy price."

"But that was their choice," said Spencer.

Laura disagreed. "Most of those soldiers were there on orders. It was their corrupt colonel that got them killed."

Acton grunted. "And he's alive and well."

"Yes. And those Bedouins, they didn't deserve to die. I agree, they shouldn't have attacked, but they were riled up by what the Russians did to their families in Libya." She shook her head. "So much hate in the world. It's a miracle we haven't destroyed ourselves by now."

Acton sighed. "Give it time. We will."

There was a tap at the door.

"Come in," said Reading.

Mitchell and Jenny stepped inside, closing the door behind them. Mitchell groaned in pleasure. "Oh, my God, it's so nice in here."

Jenny agreed. "How much does it cost to rent one of these? I want one."

Acton laughed. "You don't want to know."

She frowned. "I think we need pay raises."

Reading grunted. "You're better off buying lottery tickets."

"So, what can we do for you?" asked Acton.

Mitchell held up a sheaf of papers. "I just heard back from the German Archaeological Institute. I found out what happened."

Everyone leaned forward.

"What happened?" asked Laura eagerly.

"There's a detailed report that was filed by an SS Officer..."—he glanced at the pages—"Hauptsturmführer Heidrich Wirth. Or I guess that would be Virth."

Reading urged him on impatiently. "We'll get to German pronunciations of the letter W later. What did this report say?"

"It said that when the storm settled, the vehicles at the front of the convoy were able to pull forward. They then towed out most of the vehicles, emptied the last transport, and discovered Professor Stoltz's car entirely buried and irretrievable. They presumed the professor and his driver were entombed inside and recorded the position for later retrieval. They made it to the coast by heading to Khartoum, then redirecting back north where the cargo was loaded onto the MV Pinnau."

Laura's eyes shot wide. "You mean the tomb of Imhotep actually made it out of Egypt and to Germany?"

"Well, there's no mention of Imhotep here, though it is recorded as classified cargo. But that ship sailed on September 6, 1939, and was recorded as one of the first German losses in World War II in the Mediterranean. Sunk with all hands on board."

Acton's jaw dropped as he stared at Laura. Imhotep and the treasures buried with him, the history, all lost at the bottom of the sea, likely never to be found. All on board lost just as promised by the curse recorded in Stoltz's journal.

Eternal damnation awaits any who disturb his slumber.

Imhotep's Tomb

South of Philae, Old Kingdom

2648 BC

Neper observed the proceedings as Imhotep's mummified corpse was gently placed inside his sarcophagus. It had been decided that Imhotep's crimes couldn't be known to the public. After all, if the public were aware that a mere mortal could murder a god, that knowledge could prove catastrophic. Instead, history would record that Djoser had died peacefully in his sleep, called back by the gods to serve his people in the afterlife. No one would ever know that Imhotep had poisoned Djoser, which meant that Imhotep would be buried with full honors, though not in the crypt designated by Djoser before his death, but instead, far to the south, away from the final resting place of Imhotep's victim. The monuments in his honor and the writings forever joining the two in history would remain, however. Imhotep would be remembered with honor and reverence as advisor and trusted friend of the late pharaoh, despite the treachery.

Neper stepped forward and placed a stone tablet on Imhotep's chest, reciting what was engraved upon it, the attendants shuffling in nervous shock at the curse placed on the soul of a man buried with honors. He stepped back, the curse of the damned laid, forever preventing Imhotep from crossing into the afterlife as long as the stone remained undisturbed on his chest.

He flicked his wrist, and the attendants lifted the cover stone in place, the lid grinding loudly until it fell into its final position, forever sealing the murderer of a god into place.

"Let them in," he ordered, and one of the attendants left the tomb. A few moments later, the family entered, led by the eldest son, then his mother, followed by the rest of the children and Imhotep's other wives. They surrounded the sarcophagus, all but the eldest son weeping.

Neper withheld the traditional prayer for the dead meant to comfort the family, as there would be no prayers for Imhotep's soul today. The attendants backed away, lining up against the far wall opposite the door, their heads bowed, though it was obvious they were confused as to what was occurring.

Neper stepped forward, addressing the new head of the family. "You know what you must do?"

"Yes, sir." His lower lip trembled, the poor young man battling to control the emotions threatening to overwhelm him.

"You must speak the words as we discussed."

Imhotep's eldest glanced over at his mother and burst into tears. "I'm sorry, Mother, but I cannot, not after what you told us." He rushed into her arms and she embraced him.

"Then none of us shall renounce your father."

The son turned and placed both hands on the sarcophagus. "Forgive me, Father, for breaking my promise to you, but I never would have agreed had I known why you did what you did." He stared at Neper, a smile spreading, his chest swelling. "I am Khafra, son of Imhotep, and I will never renounce my relationship to him."

The young man's mother stepped forward, placing both her hands on the sarcophagus. "And I am Olabisi, first wife of Imhotep, mother to his eldest son, and I too shall never renounce the name Imhotep and my relationship to him."

The other children and wives joined them, echoing the pledge, and Neper stepped out of the tomb as the family chanted the name of their patriarch over and over with growing fervor. He motioned to the guards standing outside the doorway to Imhotep's final resting place and gave a curt nod to the lead guard, who snapped the order. Four of the men handed their weapons over to other members of the squad, then pushed the massive round slab into place, the doorway to the crypt slowly shrinking as the chant of "Imhotep! Imhotep!" continued unabated.

The attendants inside shouted in panic, their footfalls rapidly approaching the door. Hands reached through but spears thrust by the guards forced them back, and as the stone rolled into the keyway that would forever hold it in place finally fell silent, so did the chants and screams from those condemned to rest with Imhotep, trusted advisor to a pharaoh, best friend of a king, loving husband, devoted father.

And the best brother any little girl could hope to have.

THE END

ACKNOWLEDGMENTS

They just announced that Tina Turner died, and it reminded me of something from my youth. I'm pretty sure it was 1984 and I was in grade six. In drama class, we were given an assignment where we had to put together a ten-minute radio program.

We had to pair up. As per usual, I got a tool as a partner, but whatever. I was used to it, and accustomed to doing all the work if I wanted a good grade. I wrote the entire script, following the requirements for the assignment, including coming up with the radio station name, a sound bite for the station, a commercial, a radio play segment, and a top-forty song choice. All the prerecorded stuff was on a cassette tape, then we would have to read our script live in front of the class, pressing play and stop at strategic moments.

I called my station, "R-A-D-I-O Radio!" then played the clip from Autograph, "Turn up! The radio!" I wrote a murder mystery that had the class riveted, wanting to know what happened next, and picked a top-40 song that had to be edited down to two minutes.

I chose Tina Turner's Private Dancer.

Today I found that song playing through my head repeatedly, and memories of that day I received an A+ for my assignment flooded back, the teacher taking me aside and telling me it was the best effort he had ever heard in all the years he had been doing it.

It's amazing how songs heard decades ago can bring back memories so vividly.

As usual, there are people to thank. My dad for all the research, Niskha Kennedy for some Gen Z lingo, Brent Richards for some weapons info, and, as always, my wife, my daughter, my late mother who will always be an angel on my shoulder as I write, as well as my friends for their continued support, and my fantastic proofreading team!

To those who have not already done so, please visit my website at www.jrobertkennedy.com, then sign up for the Insider's Club to be notified of new book releases. Your email address will never be shared or sold.

Thank you once again for reading.

Made in the USA
Middletown, DE
11 July 2023

34873202R00198